THE WILD BOYS

A Space Adventure

RICK KURTIS

ISBN: 978-1-5356-1072-8

ACKNOWLEDGMENTS

I would like to take this opportunity to thank my wife, Laurii for standing by my side while I'm tucked away writing on these stories.

Also I want to thank my grandson, Ariel for helping me through this process.

And a big thank you to Deonna Miller for creating the illustrations for the front and back cover of this book. Her work and dedication is greatly appreciated.

This book is dedicated to my five children to which I am very proud to have been a part in their lives.

CONTENTS

CHAPTER ONE

IT WAS A BEAUTIFUL, PEACEFUL night. The sky was crisp, dark, and clear. The light from the stars pierced the darkness, but it was soothing, calm, and blissful. Suddenly, out of the darkness, an alien face appeared. His, head was elongated and bigger than a humans and had a yellow tint. His ears were tiny, with two canals instead of one. The veins on his forehead were protruding and had a glisten of sweat that rolled down off his brow. His face as a whole had the look of complete terror. With his flat nose, his face sunken in, and his cheeks puffed out with every breath. He was frightened, frantic, and desperate to pray, but didn't have the time. He looked down at the hole that was burnt into his side and moaned with deep pain, not just because of the injury but also for his life. His two hearts were beating hard in his chest. His eyes were very large and well dilated, revealing the reflection of what was coming toward him. His muscles started to cramp when he turned in to a field of ice meteors.

The ice chunks flew by his ship while he rocketed and dodged through the field. Some of the ice chunks exploded in front of him when they were fired upon by the three other alien ships that were in hot pursuit. The small chunks smashed into his ship, making it more difficult to maneuver.

He cringed when, all of a sudden, a laser blast ripped through his ship. The circuits and the back panel started to spark and crackle, throwing debris and smoke throughout the craft. The alien quickly grabbed an oxygen mask to put onto his face. He turned around to set some controls and saw one of the three ships closing in. When he quickly turned back around, his heart jumped up into his throat. Right in front of him was a giant ice chunk coming in fast. He quickly veered to the left, missing it by inches. The other ship that was closing in was not as lucky. It smashed into the ice wall head-on and exploded into a fiery disintegration.

The terrified alien cleared the icefield and pushed a few more buttons. Then he waited for a light to come on. The other two ships were closing in and were sighting up their target so they could fire. In an instant, all three of them pushed their buttons. The two in pursuit pushed to fire and the pursued pushed to accelerate into hyper-speed, disappearing into the darkness. The two stopped, turned, and left, leaving an empty dark space only lit up by the faraway stars. It was once again calm and peaceful.

CHAPTER TWO

THE DARKNESS STARTED TO FADE and turned into a pale-blue light in the sky. The beautiful blue sky had a few puffy clouds that danced across the sky with a gentle breeze. Down below and straight ahead was the little town of Columbus, Wisconsin, population 4,027, nestled in the rolling green hills of the United States in the early 1990s.

There were a few children flying kites, while their mothers hung up their laundry on the backyard clotheslines. Further down the way were the little shops and stores. The town's police chief, Jack Johnson, was having a malted milkshake at Brandies, the local corner drugstore.

Jack Johnson was a retired military man, born and raised in Milwaukee. After the military and two years on the police force in Milwaukee, he decided that crime there was too intense for him. So when an offer came through to be a police chief in Columbus, he jumped at the chance. Being a black man, he had to prove himself to the community. Jack loved children and had three of his own, so when it came to handling things he knew exactly what to do. He was a big man and had a deep, demanding voice, but when he laughed, it was so infectious that you couldn't help yourself but be relaxed and enjoy his company. Within one year, Jack fit in like a glove. Everyone in town loved and respected him and his family.

Continuing down the street, an innkeeper was sweeping the sidewalk in front of his store in his bright-yellow grocery apron. This was the American-dream town.

Moving further down Main Street and off to the right was the junior high and elementary school. Inside a classroom window was one particular boy, Rick Ramsey. Rick was a thin young man at the age of thirteen. His long, light-brown hair glided across his face as he sat in his chair and held his head up with his hand while he doodled on a piece of paper. The teacher was reading out of a big book while most of the kids were looking at the big brass clock on the wall, waiting for the bell to ring. The teacher looked up from her book and asked the boy who was doodling, "Rick, are you listening?"

Rick answered, "Yes, Miss Proctor, the independence of the settlers was more than just freedom from the Crown. It was…" Before Rick could continue, the school bell rang. "All right! Freedom," Rick rejoiced while he packed up his schoolbooks and papers.

Miss Proctor closed the book and added, "Turn in your assignments. Read the last chapter, and don't forget, we have a test on Monday to close out the school year. Enjoy your weekend."

All the students scattered out the door and down the hallways, chattering up a storm. Rick got to his locker, fumbled around, and took his time to put in his books. While he was packing his backpack, Mike and Chris, his two younger brothers, came running down the hall.

Chris yelled, "Rick, wait up." Rick would have waited all day, but not because of them. The boys put on their Levi's jackets. The jackets had no sleeves and silkscreen prints on the back that read "The Wild Boys." When Rick closed his locker, his girlfriend was walking up toward him. She was a beautiful tall girl with blonde hair to the middle of her back and pretty blue eyes. Her name was Jennifer Olson. She was the captain of the cheerleading squad and one of the only girls that always wore a dress to school.

Rick had a flashback to the day that he'd met Jen while she approached. The Ramseys had moved from Chicago to Columbus four years ago to get to a more relaxed place to raise five children in a country setting. Rick and Jen were in the fourth grade. A sixth-grader was teasing Jen and took her bonnet away, holding it high above his head. Rick thought it wasn't right. Being from the streets of Chicago, Rick had to handle guys like this every day, so he went over to the boy and said, "Give her back her hat."

The boy laughed, "What are you going to do about it?"

No sooner had he finished his sentence than Rick punched the boy right below the ribs, knocking out all of his air. He grabbed the bonnet when the boy buckled to the ground. "Now get out of here!" he growled. The boy gasped and trembled with fear while venturing away. Rick turned to Jen and handed her her bonnet. "I don't think he will bother you anymore," he told her. From that day on, it was true friendship.

Chris stepped up, tapping Rick on the arm, and asked, "Are you ready?" Chris put on his backpack.

Rick replied, "Just wait a minute." Then he turned to the girl. "Hi, Jen."

Jen smiled and answered, "Hi, Rick. What are you doing this weekend?"

Mike closed Rick's locker and rolled his eyes. "Ooooh-la-la," he teased, nudging Chris on the arm.

Chris said quietly to Mike, "Come on, let's go," and they walked away down the hall.

Rick answered Jen, "Nothing really. What did you have in mind?"

"There's a new movie starting at the Show Palace." She started to twist her foot and swayed shyly while she looked into Rick's eyes with love.

Rick smiled. "Okay. I'll meet you there tomorrow night at six thirty." Rick started down the hall, turned around, and started to walk backward. "Wait, what's playing?" He really didn't care; he just wanted to see her face once again and to hear her voice.

Jen put her books in her locker and turned. "Oh, another *Indiana*."

"ALLLRRRIGHTT!" Rick said with excitement, then bounded through the doors of the school. Jen closed her locker and leaned back against it with her books in her arms. She paused and smiled, dreaming of the day to come. Rick bounced down the steps, swung off the end of the rail, and headed to the bike racks. Mike and Chris were already there, waiting for him. Rick pulled out his bike and went over by his brothers. He looked at them before they left. They all did a high-five and shouted, "Wild Boys," then jumped on their bikes and headed off down the street.

They turned the corner, almost running into the police chief's car. Jack turned on the lights and tapped the siren. The boys pulled over. Jack got out of his car and walked over to them. "Now, you boys know better than that. You have to obey the stop signs just like everyone else when you're on the street."

Rick said, "Sorry, Chief Johnson, sir. We were talking about going to the movies tomorrow night and not paying attention."

Jack laughed, "Boys will be boys. Just be more careful, all right?"

Chris replied, "Yes, sir, Mister Police Chief Johnson, we will."

He took off his hat. "Now, you boys have known me for four years, just call me Jack."

Mike said, "We're not allowed to, we'll get in trouble."

Jack looked up and down the street. "Well, just between us it will be okay. Are you boys headed home? The weather station said that there is a big storm headed this way, so I'll let you go."

The boys smiled with relief, got on their bikes, and rode toward home on the outskirts of town.

CHAPTER THREE

THE CORN WAS CRISP AND high on the right side of the road. On the other side, their neighbor, Mr. Rogers, was cutting hay. Rick and Chris waved. They could smell the fresh-mowed hay as they rode up and stopped next to the field. "Hi, Mr. Rogers."

Mr. Rogers raised his sickle and drove over to the road and turned off his little Ford tractor. "Hello, boys."

Meanwhile, Mike was having trouble with the chain on his bike and he had fallen behind. "Hey, guys, wait up. My chain is caught."

Mr. Rogers got off his tractor and walked up as Mike approached. "Here, let me see that." He took out his pliers from his pocket and pulled on the chain while he turned the wheel. After a few seconds he got the chain back on the sprocket. "So, are you guys going to help me this year?"

Rick and Chris answered, "Sure."

After a few more adjustments and a few more turns with his pliers, he handed the bike back to Mike. "There you go, just like new. The chain seems to be worn out. Have your dad look at it when you get home, but I think it's time to buy a new chain," he told him.

Mike also answered, "Yeah, thanks," and took back his bike. "Um, is Wendy home?" Mike was sweet on Mr. Rogers's daughter.

Mr. Rogers smiled. "She should be by now. Probably talking on the phone, you know, like girls do, for hours and hours and hours."

Mike was now at a loss for words. "Well...do you think Wendy would want to go to the movies with Rick, Chris, Jen, and me tomorrow night? It's not a date or anything, it's just a movie."

Mr. Rogers laughed, "Well, you'll have to ask her, but I'm sure she will say yes. Either way, it's okay by me." He climbed back onto his tractor. "Yup, no problem, no problem at all. I'll give your dad a call when I need you boys to help me bale."

The boys got back on their bikes, waved, and started off again. Mike smiled. "Thanks again."

A little ways down the road, Mike's bike started to rattle. Chris turned and asked, "I thought Dad fixed that?"

"He did but I trashed it last week showing off to Wendy and I bent the sprocket."

Chris laughed, "Oh yeah, I remember that. You wiped out good."

Mike swerved his bike toward Chris. "Aw, shut up, Chris!"

Chris was the youngest of the three, at the tender age of ten. He was everyone's friend, open and funny and always eager to help in whatever he could do. All the other kids in his class seemed to gravitate toward him.

Mike, on the other hand, was a stocky young boy who was very outgoing. He loved to dance and sing but had his prankish side that was wild and free. He was also very smart and quick to learn, soaking up knowledge like a sponge. When they were all together, people would say they were triplets of different sizes.

CHAPTER FOUR

JUST THEN, THE BOYS HEARD a loud piercing noise in the fluffy clouds above, and an object streaked down from the sky. It dropped at first almost straight down, then made a radical turn, leveled off, and crashed into the woods about half a mile in front of them. They could almost see the trees move when the sky over the woods filled with all the birds. The boys ducked and came to a complete stop to look. By the time they had stopped, it had crashed.

Chris pointed. "Look! What was that?"

Rick answered, "A plane, maybe?"

Mike replied, "No. It couldn't be a plane. It moved in way too fast and leveled off too quick."

Rick pushed off on his pedal. "Come on, let's go see."

They rushed off on their bikes and headed down the road. Rick was in the lead and rode down into the ditch to pop out on the other side onto a tractor path that led to the woods. The other two followed close behind until they got to the old stone bridge. They parked their bikes so they could start to look. Their hearts were beating with excitement as they entered into the woods. The woods were thick with an abundance of green foliage. Some birds were calling and the branches in the trees were creaking while the squirrels rustled throughout them. Chris picked a few big ripe blackberries on the way and ate them. Mike found a well-tuned stick and used it to thrash through the thicket. Rick decided to climb up a tree, to get a better view.

Mike hollered while he hit the ground with the stick, "It's going to get dark soon. There are some heavy clouds rolling in."

Rick looked down from the tree and announced, "Yeah, and you should see them from up here."

Chris yelled back, really excited, "Over here! I found it, over here!" He waited for the other two, and waved his arms to signal them so they could see him.

Rick climbed down from the tree and started toward him. "Where?" he yelled.

Chris hollered again, "Here! Over here!"

Rick ran into Mike and Mike pointed. "There he is." They saw Chris waving his arms, jumping up and down. When they came up to Chris, they could see the crash site come into view. A blank look of awe came upon their faces. "Wow," Rick said.

Mike stared. "Whoa!"

Walking into the crash area, they had to climb over and under a few fallen trees. There were about ten trees that were sheared off, mangled, or maimed. There were pieces of craft and glass-string wire stretched out all over the place. The main body of the ship had bounced into the ground and out, leaving a deep hole. It had come to rest tilted upright against a big oak tree. The boys climbed through the mess to get to the hull of the ship on the passenger side. They wanted to see if there were any survivors.

They all walked up to the ship on the right-hand side of the vessel. The hatch was broken open, leaving the control panels and the seats visible. They could see all the instruments but no victims. All they found was this yellow oil-like stuff splattered about the left side of the cockpit.

Chris looked at the craft. "Hey, bucket seats." He climbed in, sat in the passenger seat on the right, tapped the instrument panels, and grabbed the stick.

Rick scratched his head. "Where's the pilot? Someone had to be flying this thing."

Mike went to look in the woods past the oak tree. "Maybe he flew out over here?"

Rick started around the back side of the ship and examined it as he went. Chris turned to look back at Rick. "Maybe it was unmanned." Just then a long arm with a big wide hand reached over from the left side of the craft and grabbed Chris's arm. It was covered with the sticky yellow oil and attached to the crash victim. Chris turned back to look and screamed in terror, "Hey! Let go." But the hand didn't let go.

Mike came running around from the back side of the tree. Rick came around to the left side from the rear. They saw this mangled body with what looked like a yellow pumpkin on its shoulders. Rick reached over and put his hand on the alien's shoulder to pull him away. The alien let go of Chris and turned back around in terrifying pain. Chris jumped out of the seat and stared at the alien.

The alien started to babble in an unknown language. His face had the look of urgency and concern on it. It was like he was trying to plead to the boys. Rick knelt down to see if he could help. The alien put his hand on Rick's shoulder and babbled on some more. Then he turned and reached into the ship behind the seat. The alien pulled out a chrome briefcase. After he handed it to Rick, he pointed at himself, then at the sky, still babbling. The alien reached into his spacesuit and pulled out a two-inch round metallic disk with holes in it and handed it to Rick. He coughed up some yellow oil, dropped his arm, and pointed at the case, then at the disk. Then he reached out and pulled on Mike's hand, placing it on top of the case with his own. The case lit up and the light faded away when Mike pulled his hand back off. The alien said some more words that the boys couldn't understand, and then he slumped over and was dead.

Mike was the first to speak. "Whoa! I wonder where he is from."

Chris was next. "I don't know, but he got this yellow oil all over my arm."

Rick answered, "That's not oil. It's this guy's blood."

Chris grabbed a bunch of leaves and started to wipe down his arm. "Ooo, eee, aaa, yeak!"

Mike thought out loud, "We have to tell the police. No, the Air Force!"

Rick turned to Mike. "Are you kidding?" he said with a wrinkled forehead.

"What?"

"Do you think they would believe us? The Wild Boys? I mean, come on, the ones who played that prank on them with our clubhouse last year?"

Mike thought about it and flashed back in his mind. About a year ago, their father had built them a playhouse of an unusual size and shape. The boys anonymously called their neighbor, which in turn made the neighbor call for the authorities. The authorities called the military and the military called the Air Force and they all showed up together. Their little prank had turned into a big fiasco and the boys were grounded for a month. "Oh yeah, I forgot about that. Then what should we do? This is real and he is right here."

Chris came up with an idea. "I know, let's wait until dark. Then we can tell Dad that we saw something crash or something. Dad will call the cops and we'll be in the clear. I mean, the guy's dead, he's not going anywhere, so when they find him, we'll be in the clear. We might even be heroes, because this one's a true story."

Mike agreed, "Yeah! We might even get into the paper and maybe even get an award or something." He picked up the case. "We'll put the case back in the ship so they can find it."

Rick grabbed the case from Mike. "No! He gave that case and this disk to us. Didn't you see the look on his face? Didn't you hear the tone in his voice of what he was trying to say? I know we didn't understand it, but I could feel it. He wanted us to protect these things. The only thing that they will do is trash them or tear them apart, analyzing them. No, we're taking the case and the disk with us. They will find the ship and our dead friend, that's good enough." Rick took the shoelace out of his shoe, put it through the hole of the disk, and tied it around his neck.

A cool chill came into the air. Chris looked up into the sky and felt sprinkles of rain fall upon his face. The wind started to blow the trees. Chris said, "It's starting to rain, guys. We'd better get home."

Rick grabbed the case. "All right, let's go." And they all headed back to their bikes on the old stone bridge.

CHAPTER FIVE

THE BOYS RACED HOME WITH Rick in the lead. Rick rode around to the back side of the house. Chris and Mike came sliding into the bike rack at about the same time. Rick came around the house and they all jumped off their bikes and ran into the house. *Bang* went the screen door.

Their mom was at the kitchen stove preparing supper for her hungry men when she saw them come in. "Where have you boys been all day?" she said with a harsh voice, trying to cover up the nervousness from her worry about them.

Jenna, their little sister, was sitting at the table. "Yeah."

Rick answered, "Riding around town."

Mike spoke up with Rick. "Just bumming around all over the place."

Chris spoke up at the same time. "Down by the creek."

Mom gave them a look. "Aha… Well, just don't stand there, go wash up for supper." The boys took off. "Don't make a mess, I just cleaned up there," she hollered.

The boys headed up the stairs while their mom was still mumbling on, which they never listened to anyway. They were still too excited about this afternoon's discovery and were whispering back and forth to themselves.

Chris asked, "Where did you put the case?"

Rick answered, "Ssshhh, keep it down. It's out back, under our window."

When they reached the top of the stairs, their other sister, Bree, came out of her room. She put her hands on her hips and gave them stern look. "Where have you guys been? Mommy has been worried all day. All of you guys are going to be in big trouble." All the while she spoke with a giggle in her throat.

Bree and Jenna were identical twins at the precocious age of six. If they stood on each side of a doorway, it would look as though each one was looking into a mirror. The boys loved their sisters but picked on them unmercifully, so if the girls could get the boys into trouble, they were always glad to help.

Chris turned to answer. "None of your business, and we aren't in any trouble!" he said, sticking out his tongue. They all walked away from Bree and went into the bathroom.

While they were washing up, they looked out the bathroom window and noticed a truck coming up the wide paved road. Mike said, "Dad's home." The boys quickly dried their hands, leaving half the dirt on the towel, and ran down the stairs. Like a well-timed clock, the boys rounded the corner, almost knocking into their mother just when she started to say, "It's time to eat. Oh, watch where you're going. Go and sit down." Then she went to the door to greet her man.

Joe pulled up into the driveway, stopped and looked at his watch, and smiled. He thought back to the days when they lived in the inner city of Chicago. Joe and his wife, Lisa, had lived in a three-bedroom apartment on the fourth floor. Lisa was a beautiful, thin blonde with bright green eyes who'd given up her modeling career to raise their five children. They were so worried every day when the boys went to school and Joe was working from sunup to sundown. Some days he wouldn't see his family at all. He remembered why they left, after their apartment building was raided and locked down for a whole day. That was when they'd had enough and decided to move to the country. Joe had landed a job as an aerospace technician. Moving to the country was the best decision for his children and his wife. He looked out his truck window at the clubhouse that he'd made for the boys, and then at the bike rack where all the children's bikes were lined up, and smiled, stepping out of the truck. "Daddy's home," he shouted.

Joe walked in through the kitchen door. The twins started to sing, "Daddy's home, Daddy's home." Joe hugged each of the girls while they hung on his legs. Then he kissed them and sent them to the table. He leaned over and kissed his wife before going over to the kitchen sink to wash up for supper. "Hi, dear. Did you have a nice day?"

Lisa answered, "Yeah. How about you, long day, hon?"

Joe dried his hands and said with a growl in his voice, "Oh, don't ask."

Lisa turned. "Well, we could always move back to Chicago."

Rick voiced up, "Oh no we're not. I'll run away first."

Joe answered, "Yeah, me too. I didn't mean it like that." He turned to his wife and put his hands around her waist. "Hey, you'd better get your clothes in off the line and batten down the hatches. There's a big storm that followed me all the way home." Joe sat down at the table and patted Chris on the head. "Chris, go make sure everything is put away outside and the garage door is locked up while your mother is getting her clothes off the line." Chris jumped up from the table, always willing to be helpful, and quickly ran outside.

Lisa grabbed the laundry basket. "Bree, when we get back in, it is your turn to say grace tonight."

Bree was excited and eager to say grace. "Hurry back, Mommy. Maybe Chris will help you carry the clothes in. He's faster at that." Lisa laughed and went out the door with her basket.

Joe sat at the table and asked, "So, what have you boys been up to today?" Before either of the two boys could answer, the girls started talking about how their mom had been so worried.

Jenna spoke up first. "Mommy was worried about the boys because they came home late today."

Then Bree chimed in, "Yeah. She said if they weren't home in ten minutes they were going to be grounded for a month. Then they came home two minutes later. Yeah, too bad!" She stuck her tongue out at the two boys at the table.

Just then Chris came into the house through the side door, carrying the laundry basket full of the day's clean laundry. Lisa followed right behind, struggling with the screen door while the wind tried to pull it out of her hands. She closed the screen door and then the house door. "Whoa, it's a-coming. I could see it is already pouring at the Rogers' place, and he just mowed all that hay today, too. Chris, you can leave that basket by the stairs and come and sit down for supper." Lisa sat down and Chris came back into the room and sat. "Bree, you can begin grace now."

Everyone folded their hands and bowed their heads. "Dear Lord, Father in heaven, thank you for this food that we are about to receive. Bless it and let it nourish our bodies the way your word nourishes our soul. In Jesus's name we pray, Amen."

All the kids dug in as the food was passed around the table. Joe started the night's family conversation. "So Lisa, my love, how was your day?"

Lisa smiled with a gleam at her husband while she passed the mashed potatoes. "Oh, same old, same old. Mary did let me set up the display window today, and five people walked in and commented on how nice it looked." All the kids clapped and cheered. Lisa smiled and took a little bow. "Thank you, thank you very much."

Joe replied, "Well good, maybe Mary will realize what you do for that place with all your hard work and maybe, just maybe, she will give you a raise."

Lisa smirked. "Yeah, sure, when monkeys fly out..."

Joe interrupted and the kids all snickered. "Okay, what did you guys do today, Mike?"

Mike swallowed his mashed potatoes. "I got an A in math and..."

The girls started to talk over the top of Mike. Bree and Jenna talked at the same time. Bree said, "Daddy, Daddy, look at what we did," while Jenna said, "Look at what I did."

Joe continued to acknowledge Mike. "Well, very good, Mike. Very good."

Then Lisa nudged Joe. "Dear, pay attention to what the girls want to tell you. They've been waiting all day to show you what they did." She pointed her finger to the refrigerator and the girls jumped up from their chairs to point out their own personal pictures. Their chairs were nearly knocked over when they ran to pull their pictures off the fridge. They brought them over to their dad.

Joe looked the pictures over and grinned. "Wow! These are really nice."

Jenna pointed. "This one's mine."

Then Bree said, "And I made this one."

Joe smiled. "I can see that. You two are so talented."

Lisa interjected, "All right, girls, sit back down and tell Daddy about your spelling test at school today."

The girls returned to their chairs and Bree said, "Oh yeah, I got one hundred percent."

Jenna sat down and boasted, "Me too, Daddy. I got one hundred percent too and I got a gold star." She looked at her twin sister and stuck out her tongue. "Ha!"

Joe smiled. "Well, well, well, my, my, my, that is excellent. I am so very proud of both of you. How about you, Chris?"

Chris wasn't too enthused about talking because this was his favorite meal to eat. "Oh, I did okay I guess."

Joe continued around the table. "Rick, what's new with you?"

Rick replied while he pulled at his mashed potatoes, "Oh, nothing."

"Oh nothing? What do you mean, oh nothing? How was school today?"

Rick answered, "Boring."

"Boring, how come?" Joe asked.

"Oh, Miss Snootypants Proctor wants us to do a hundred-word problem in math over the weekend."

Joe snarled, "Oooooh, that old hag-a-muffin, I'll bet she just lives to torture you kids. Are you going to do it?"

"I have already done it."

Joe smiled. "Oh yeah, that's my boy."

Rick continued, "Yeah, I did them during her history lecture on, and I quote, 'The Declaration of Independence in correlation with the bicentennial of the United States,'" he said in a monotone voice. Then he added, "Oh, Dad, we're thinking about going to the movies tomorrow night. Can you take us?"

Joe smiled. "Sure, I don't see why not."

Mike voiced up, "Yeah, I bet he was thinking about Jen in history class."

Rick turned with the reply, "Oh yeah, what about Wendy?"

All the kids started to chatter back and forth, getting louder and louder. After about a minute, Lisa decided to step in. "All right, settle down." The banter continued. "I said that's enough, Chris, Rick, Mike, girls." They didn't hear her. She looked over at Joe. "Will things ever change? Joe, do something."

Now Joe was a man of very little discipline, but he did have a system that the kids knew very well. When Joe started to count, if he got to number three, he would stand up and take action. That was something they didn't want to see or be a part of. Joe smirked; then, with a stern look, he replied, "All right, kids, that's enough. One, two..." Before he could say three, a huge lightning bolt and the sound of thunder cracked over the house.

The house shook so much that the cabinet doors rattled and a pan fell out onto the floor. It looked like the bolt of lightning came right through the house over their heads. Everyone ducked, including Lisa and the girls, who let out a scream. Mike threw his mashed potatoes up into the air and Chris spilled his orange juice. Then everybody paused for a moment.

Mike, being the smart whip that he was, was the first one who spoke. "Okay, Dad, you don't have to be so dramatic, we get the point." Everyone had a chuckle and quickly finished eating so they could watch the rain come down. A few more loud cracks of thunder came across the air.

They all got up from the table and went to the door to look out. The raindrops started to fall while they watched. In the distance, they could see sheets of rain coming across the fields. Lisa said, "Oh my gosh, here it comes." The rain started to come down harder and the wind started blowing it through the screen door. Lisa closed the door and turned to clear the table. Everyone else started to go into the living room.

Joe started to walk away with the kids. "I told you it was coming."

Lisa cleared her throat. "Ahem. Aren't we forgetting something?"

Rick was the first to turn around. "Oh yeah." They all made a U-turn back to the kitchen to help clear off the table. Once it was done, they headed back to the living room to watch some television.

While the children and Joe were watching TV, the boys started to talk back and forth among themselves in soft voices so no one could hear them, or so they thought.

"Now?"

"No, not yet."

"When?"

"Wait."

"Maybe if we…."

Joe broke into the boys' conversation during a commercial. "If you guys aren't going to be quiet so the rest of us can hear the television, go watch the TV up in your room."

Rick nudged his brothers. "Yeah, good idea. Let's go, guys." So the boys jumped up and went running full speed up to their room. *Bang* went the bedroom door. The girls started to clap, happy that it was just them and their daddy watching television. Joe put a finger to his mouth to quiet the girls and the girls climbed up onto their daddy's lap.

When the boys got into their room, they locked the bedroom door and jumped on their beds. Rick went over and pulled out his junk box that he had hidden under the foot of his bed. He started to dig through all the stuff that he had saved and hidden away. The rain was still coming down and it seemed to be getting stronger. The other two boys were anxiously waiting to tell their dad what they'd seen and couldn't stop from fidgeting while waiting for Rick. They pushed and pulled at each other while they waited.

Rick spoke up. "Will you guys stop it? You're making too much noise. Mom is going to come up here and we'll get in trouble and have to go to bed." The two settled down a little, knowing that Rick was right. They sat and watched, wondering what Rick was so eagerly searching for.

Chris said, "Rick, stop playing in that junk box and let's go tell Dad what we saw. It's getting late."

Mike was also ready. "Chris is right. He could be going to sleep before we have a chance to tell him. Hurry up, let's go tell him now."

Rick continued to dig through the box. "We'll wait about five more minutes or so then we can run down to tell him that we saw a plane crash."

Chris asked, "Plane crash, where?"

Rick knocked Chris on the side of his shoulder. "Where? In the woods, you dummy. It was your idea."

Chris scratched his head. "Oh yeah."

Mike sat on the bed and watched. "What are you digging for, China?"

Rick pulled out a long string, half rolled up on a stick. While he was untangling it from the other junk, Chris started to help him to pull it out. He reached over to his nightstand and grabbed the scissors and snipped the tangled mess away.

Rick told him, "Chris, get me a coat hanger, a wire one."

Chris went to the closet and pulled out a hanger with a shirt on it and handed it to Rick. "Here you go. I couldn't find an empty one." Rick pulled off the shirt and threw it toward Mike.

Mike balled up the shirt and threw it back into the closet on the floor. "Oh well, I didn't like that shirt anyway."

Rick bent the coat hanger into a hook and tied the string onto one end. Then he headed to the window. Mike jumped off the bed and went to the window while Rick was opening it. The rain was coming down hard, straight down. Rick stuck his head out and started to lower the string with the hook on the end made from the hanger. "I can't see. Get me a flashlight." Mike reached over to the dresser and grabbed his flashlight. He turned it on and stuck his head out the window with Rick. Chris felt left out and bounced back and forth on Rick's and Mike's backs trying to see what they were doing. "Chris! Back off!" Rick said angrily while he waved his hand behind him. Chris backed off with a huffy look on his face. He bounced on the bed with his arms crossed.

Rick hooked the case and started to pull it up and it hit the side of the house. With the pounding rain, he was hoping that no one heard it. "I got it! Help me pull it up." Chris grabbed the string while Rick leaned out the window some more to hold the case away from the house so it wouldn't bang again. Mike held on to Rick. "Careful, careful, hold it!"

Rick reached down to grab the case by the handle. Mike grabbed Rick by his pants and Chris grabbed his feet. "Pull me in, pull me in." When they pulled him in, his pants started to give way; then his shoe came off and Chris fell on his backside. Mike quickly grabbed Rick by the middle of his shirt and jerked him up into the room. Mike and Rick fell back on the floor with the case.

"Whew!" Mike got up and went to the bathroom and got some towels. Chris stuck his head out of the window just to get it wet so he didn't feel left out. When he pulled his head back in and turned around, Mike threw a towel into his face. "Thanks." They all dried off and knelt down in the center of the room around the case, drying it off with their towels. They started to look it over and figure out how to open it.

Mike put his hand on top to see if it would glow again. It didn't. "How do you open this thing?"

Rick picked the case up and stood it up on end. "I don't know, but it's time to go tell Dad." He picked the case up and hid it in the back corner of the closet. They all put on dry T-shirts and started for the door. "Now remember, we just saw it happen and it looked like a plane." The boys opened the door and went running downstairs, all excited. You would have thought that the roof was falling in. The boys announced, "Dad! Dad!"

Joe jumped up from his easy chair, half asleep. "What?"

Mike started, "We saw something crash into the woods!"

Chris added, "Yeah!"

Rick answered, "It looked like a plane."

Joe got up and rubbed his eyes. "Are you sure?"

The boys replied, "Yes, really!"

Lisa came in from the other room. "What are you boys babbling about?"

Joe said, "The boys said they saw a plane crash into Abanie Woods."

Lisa crossed her arms. "Is that what all that banging was up in your room, a plane crash? And how come all three of you have wet heads?"

Joe got up and walked over to the telephone.

The boys answered, "No, really!"

Rick said, "It came down when we were looking out the window at the rain."

Lisa turned and looked at Chris. "Oh really, Chris, is that true?"

Chris swallowed hard. "Well, I didn't see it, Rick did."

Joe dialed the phone. The phone was answered by an operator. "911 emergency, how can I help you?"

Joe answered, "Yeah, this is Joe Ramsey. My sons said they just saw a plane go down in Abanie Woods."

The operator said, "Are you at home right now at 3003 Ricky Road?"

"Yes we are. Abanie Woods is about half a mile south of our house."

"I have a patrol car dispatched on the way to your location. They will need you to repeat your statement for their report. Can you describe what your sons witnessed?"

"Well, hang on, I'll give you one of my boys that saw the crash. Here, Rick, tell her what you saw."

Rick got on the phone. "Hello."

The operator said, "Hello, Rick, can you tell me what you saw tonight?"

"Well, it looked like an airplane. It swooped down and went into the woods."

"Was it a big plane or a small plane?"

"It looked like a small plane, maybe with two props."

"Okay, was it on fire or anything like that?"

"No, it just looked like it was out of control."

"Thank you, young man. Please put your father back on the line." Rick handed the phone back to his dad. "Sir, emergency crews should be there in about ten to fifteen minutes. If your son can remember anything else, please let the crew know, all right? Being that it's not at your house, there is no need for me to continue on the phone. Thank you, sir, and have a safe night."

Joe replied before she hung up, "Tell them that I'll wait for them down by the woods in my truck. It might save some time."

"All right, sir, thank you. Goodbye."

Joe hung up the phone and went to the closet and Lisa asked, "So where do you think you're going?"

Joe grabbed his raincoat and looked out the kitchen door. "Well, we called it in. So we should be there to help." He pecked Lisa on the cheek. "Besides, I think it stopped raining outside."

The kids all pleaded, "Can we go? Can we go too, please?"

Joe looked at the girls. "You stay here with your mother." The boys got all excited and headed for the closet.

Lisa sternly said, "Oh no! You boys aren't going anywhere. It's time for bed."

The boys cried, "But Mommmm!" Rick threw his boots back into the closet.

She pointed to the stairs. "No buts about it, unless you want them red."

The twins sang with laugher, "Ha, ha, ha, ha, ha."

Joe walked out the door, not saying anything because of the tone of Lisa's voice. Rick went to the door to talk to his dad. "Dad, I think it's on the left side of the old stone bridge, probably about a hundred yards in."

Lisa pulled Rick back inside and then said to Joe, "You be careful, Joe."

Joe pecked her on the cheek. "I will." He walked over to his truck. *Bang* went the truck door and *vroom* went the engine, and off he went down the road to wait by the turnoff at the tractor path.

The boys went into the living room to watch out the window. About five minutes went by when they heard the sirens. They could see the flashing lights coming down the road. The police car went whizzing past the house, followed by the fire truck paramedic unit, then the rest of the firemen crew. Rick replied, "There goes Jack!"

Lisa came into the room. "All right, you three go upstairs and get ready for bed, and don't forget to take a shower and brush your teeth." All the boys ran upstairs to take a shower and to put on their PJs. They didn't want to miss any of the action. They sat in their room and looked out the window. The wind started to pick back up and it started to rain again.

Mike said, "I wonder when Dad is going to be home? He's been gone for about an hour."

Just then, Chris said, "Look, there they come."

The boys could see the headlights of the trucks coming down the road. They went running back downstairs to hear the news. They stood by the door and waited with their mother. Joe came in soaking wet from head to toe. The boys were all excited and all said at the same time, "Dad! Dad! Did you find it? Did you see it?"

Joe took off his raincoat and sat down to slip out of his boots. "See what?"

Chris quickly replied, "See the ship." Before he could say anymore, Rick grabbed Chris by the mouth, muffling his next sentence.

Rick said, "The crash. Did you find the crash site?"

Joe got up to put his boots away. "No, we didn't find anything. It was too dark and it started to rain again." The boys looked really disappointed. "Jack said he would come back out at the break of day to try again."

Mike asked, "Can we go with you tomorrow, please?"

Chris quickly added, "Please, Dad, can we?"

"Well, first light is at six, are you going to be ready?"

Rick answered, "Yeah, we'll be ready."

The boys started to give their dad a hug and he said, "Okay then, you'd better get to bed now."

Chris was the first to say, "Okay, good night." All three said good night and their mom gave them each a kiss and they headed out of the room.

While they were walking away, Joe said, "Good night, boys. I'll be up in a little bit."

The boys headed up the stairs off to bed while their dad sat back down in the kitchen and Lisa rubbed his shoulders. Then she asked, "So you didn't find anything?"

"Nope."

Lisa continued, "I wonder what they're up to?"

"Why do you say that?"

"Well, the more I thought about it, they were acting weird all night. I thought they were just excited about the weekend being here."

"Well, maybe they are. Five more days and they have the whole summer. I mean, it's really not like them to pull a prank like that again. Not right before summer at least."

"I guess you're right, but I still think they're up to something. You'd better go tuck in the girls or they will have a fit. I love having you home at night."

Joe got up and gave his wife a peck on the cheek. "Yeah, me too." Joe went upstairs to say his good-nights. He tucked in the girls, then went to the boys' room to say good night. "Good night, guys. Bright and early at six o'clock, that's when Jack said he would come back out."

When Joe walked out the door, Rick got up and followed him to the stairs. "Dad?"

"What, Rick?"

"Did you look to the left side of the bridge, over by the big oak tree?"

"I don't know, Rick. We had fifteen men out there combing the woods. We'll see tomorrow in the light of day. Now go to bed."

"Okay, night, Dad."

"Good night."

CHAPTER SIX

FIVE THIRTY A.M. CAME ALL too soon for Joe and Lisa, but not for the boys. Their radio alarm blared, rattling the whole house. All three boys jumped from their beds and rushed to put on their clothes. Once they were dressed, they went running down the stairs to wake up their dad.

Rick said excitedly, "Come on, Dad, we're going to be late."

Lisa opened one eye and turned her head. Joe got up after Lisa nudged him and started to put on his pants. He yawned and sat on the edge of the bed. "I know, I know."

Lisa looked up, still half asleep. "Do you want me to make you some breakfast first?"

"No, I'll have the boys back before nine o'clock, if we find anything or not."

Joe leaned over and kissed Lisa on the nose. She turned her head and plumped it back down onto the pillow. "Good, good night."

Joe went to the kitchen to put on his shoes, where the boys were waiting for him and were raiding the refrigerator. "You guys go get your boots on if you want to go along. It's still going to be plenty wet outside." The boys ran to the closet and the twins came into the kitchen. They yawned and rubbed their eyes and climbed onto their daddy's lap.

Bree asked, "Can we go too?"

Joe smiled and kissed her on the cheek. "No, sweetheart, you two have to stay home with Mommy." He gave them both a peck on the cheek and sent them off to his bedroom. They walked into the master bedroom and crawled into bed with Lisa. The boys started to fight in the closet. Rick watched while Chris tried to find his boots. Joe got up and started to head out the door. "Let's go, guys." Outside he went.

Chris grabbed his boots and Rick pulled him out of the way. "Come on, Chris, move."

Chris and Mike put on their boots and headed out the door. "Come on!" Mike said.

Rick grabbed his boots at the same time that Joe honked the horn. *Beep, beep.* "Well, wait," he said while digging through the floor of the closet.

Chris yelled, "Let's go."

Rick ran out of the house with his boots in his hand. "All right." They all jumped into the truck and

Joe drove down the road to the tractor path to wait for the police chief.

Joe looked into the rearview mirror and saw Jack coming down the road. "Here he comes, right on time." He glanced over at Chris, looking at his boots. "Ah, Chris?"

"Yeah, Dad."

"Your boots are on the wrong feet."

Chris looked down at his feet. "Oh yeah."

Joe got out of the truck when the police chief pulled up behind him. Jack opened the car door and stepped out. "Good morning, Joe."

"Morning, Jack."

"Well, you want to try again?"

"At least we can see now."

"Yeah. I see you brought the troops with you."

The boys all yelled out of the truck, "Hi, Jack!"

Joe gave them all a stern look. "Boys!"

Jack smiled. "Hi, guys." He gave a chuckle and put his hand on Joe's shoulder. "It's okay, Joe, I told them they could call me Jack. We're all men here. Now, do you think with the boys' help we'll find anything today?"

Joe answered, "Yeah, they know these woods like the back of their hands. My truck is a four-wheel-drive and we can take it back to the bridge. That's where Rick said he saw it go down."

Jack felt his hip. "Okay then, let me call in first and get my radio." Jack went to make his call, while Joe went back to the truck. "347 to base. 347 to base."

Marie, the station's operator, got on the horn. "Go ahead, Jack, over."

"Yeah, Marie, I'm going to be away from the car for a while looking for the plane crash in Abanie Woods, so I'll be on my mobile, over."

"10-4, Jack."

Jack came around to the passenger side of the truck and hopped in. "Hi, Chris," Jack said while Chris scooted over to make more room.

Chris replied, "Hi, Chief Johnson."

Joe put the truck into four-wheel-drive and drove down the slippery tractor path. Jack turned around to talk to the other boys. "I see you guys came to help."

Rick said, "Yeah. I know right where it is."

Jack looked at Rick, trying to hold on as the truck slid around. "Oh really, how do you know?"

Joe splashed and slid while he drove through the puddles of mud. "Yeah, he's the one that saw it from his bedroom window."

Jack questioned Rick, "You could see it all the way from your house?"

Rick had to think of something fast. "Well, I was looking out the window with the binoculars that Dad gave us." By that time, Joe had stopped the truck on the bridge. As soon as the doors opened, the boys started to run off. Joe yelled, "Hang on there, guys." They all stopped and came back to the truck.

Jack said, "Now, you guys are my deputies, and we are going to do this right. Let's double up. Chris will go with me and you two stick within eyesight of your father. Now, you guys head off in that direction and Chris and I will search off this way." He pointed out toward the woods.

Rick led the way for his group on the right side of the creek while Chris and Jack headed off into the thicket on the other side. Chris pulled on Jack's arm while he was trying to look. "No Jack, it's this way."

Jack gave a little chuckle. "Yeah? Oh, sorry, Chris, I didn't know you were a master detective now."

Rick went straight to the crash site with Mike and their dad right behind. Rick saw the big oak tree. His heart started to beat fast, excited about seeing the ship again. He yelled out, "Here it is! There's the big oak tree and there's the…" A big pause set in while Joe walked up and looked over the ripped-up broken trees.

Rick and Mike looked at each other and Joe yelled, "Jack! Over here, quick."

Jack and Chris came in from the other side. When they reached the site, Chris said, "There it is."

Jack walked in and looked around. "There what is?"

Rick replied, "It's gone!"

Joe asked, "What's gone?"

Rick continued, "It was here. I know it was. See the hole in the ground and, and the big oak tree? See how it is all skinned up?"

Mike added, "Yeah, look at all these trees. They're all twisted and broken."

Jack walked in to look for the evidence. "Well, well, well. Let's just wait a minute here and think." He walked around and looked at all the trees, and then up at the big oak tree and felt where the bark was ripped off. "Yeah, it sure does look like something crashed here." Jack walked around and looked more. "This could be it."

Joe took his cap off and scratched his head. "Then where's the plane? Did it just dissolve with the rain?"

Jack turned to Rick and asked, "Rick, exactly what did you see last night?"

Now Rick had to come up with something new. "Well, I, I don't exactly know now. I thought it was a plane or something."

Jack walked over to where the broken trees were and leaned back against one with a puzzled look on his face. "I've seen things like this before." He paused. "Rick, what you probably saw was either ball lightning or a tornado touch-down."

Rick scoffed, "Yeah, right."

Jack continued, "No, really. It happens all the time. You see, sometimes a big ball of lightning rolls down from the sky and smash, bang, crash, just like a bowling ball into the pins. Then it either fizzles out or rolls up again. Or, a tornado tail, it starts out high in the dark clouds and will quickly drop down, smash up a few things, and then bounce back up into the clouds. So, in all the excitement of the storm and the lightning and all, you just assumed that it was a plane."

Rick didn't want to be caught in a lie, so he just stood there and nodded his head. "Yeah, I guess so."

Jack pulled his radio from his hip. "We'll check around some more, but I think we found our crash site." Then he got on the radio. "347 to base. 347 to base."

"Go ahead, Jack. I read you loud and clear, over."

"Marie, did we get any other calls on a crash or a missing plane, over?"

"No, Jack, negative, over."

"Okay, do me a favor and call the airports and ask them if they had anything run off the radar last night, just to double check, over."

"10-4, Jack."

Thinking they'd found their crash site, Joe and Jack went off in one direction and the boys headed off in another. Mike turned to Rick and asked, "What do we do now?"

Rick replied, "We keep our mouths shut."

Chris walked backward in front of them. "But where did it go?"

Rick replied again, "How in the heck should I know?"

The boys could hear Jack's radio off in the distance while he received a call from the office. "Base to 347, Jack. Base to 347, Jack."

"Yeah, Marie, go ahead, over."

"I called the airports and they had no planes in the area. All personnel were grounded due to the storm coming in. They had nothing to report, over."

"10-4. We're about to wrap it up here, over."

"10-4, Jack. Say, stop by the Martins' on your way in. His car died again, over."

"Sure thing, Marie. 10-4, over and out." Then the boys heard him call out, "Come on, guys, let's wrap it up and call it a day."

When they got back up to the truck, Joe took off his boots and put them in the back of the truck. "You boys take your boots off before you get into the truck. I don't want mud all over the seats."

Rick asked, "Can we just ride in the back?"

Joe smirked. "Yeah, sure, I don't care, hop in." The boys jumped into the back of the truck while their dad and Jack got back in and Joe turned the truck around in the mud. "Hang on, boys," he said before he rolled up the window. He pulled over to one side, floored the truck, and spun it around, throwing the mud high up in the air and all over.

CHAPTER SEVEN

WHEN THE BOYS GOT HOME, they washed off the mud with the garden hose before going into the house. They entered all disappointed and bewildered. It was about eight o'clock and Lisa and the girls greeted them by the door. The boys put their boots in the closet and sluggishly walked up the stairs to wash up for breakfast. They didn't utter a word.

Lisa gave them a stern look as they walked in the door. Joe came in next. Lisa asked, "Well, did you find anything today?"

"Yeah, nothing but a hole in the woods."

"Well, I sure did."

"What did you find?"

"Oh, you'll see, wash up now and come and eat breakfast first."

Moments later, the boys came down the stairs and started to enter the kitchen. Lisa eyed Lisa the boys and walked over to the stove. Bree and Jenna laughed at the boys while they came through the door. Jenna said, "Boy, are you guys gonna get it." Bree smirked at the boys.

The boys sat down at the table and Mike said to the twins, "Shut up, girls."

Lisa turned from the stove and came over to the table. "Girls, that's enough now. It's time to say grace and eat. Jenna, say the blessing, please."

"Dear Father in heaven, thank you for this food we are about to receive. Bless this food and let it nourish our bodies the way your word nourishes our soul. In Jesus's name we pray, Amen."

Everyone ate without saying anything except the usual morning table-talk. The boys said very little, not really knowing what to say. Mom finished first and left the room for a little while. No one really noticed that she had gone.

She came back in and stood in the doorway of the kitchen. "Is everyone about done?" Joe went to grab the last biscuit but put it back when he heard the tone in her voice. "Well, good, would one of you boys care to explain where you got this?" She pulled out the chrome case from behind the door and held it in front of her to show the boys. "I found this in their closet with some dirty clothes." There was a long pause. The boys got all red in the face. The hairs stood up on the backs of their necks and tingled while the prickly heat rushed through their heads. "Well?"

Mike spoke up. "It's mine. I mean, it is Johnny Marshall's. I traded him my skateboard for it."

Lisa answered, "Yeah, really? Then why is your skateboard still on the porch?"

"I'm going to take it to him on Monday at school."

Lisa looked the case over. "This case sure looks awfully expensive. I think I'll just call Johnny's mother to make sure it's all right." She went over to pick up the phone.

Mike sat up but didn't want to press too hard, so he tried to plead. "No! I mean, it's all right. His dad gave him his old case because the latches were broken and Johnny didn't use it. Rick has his junk box and Chris has his toy box. I just wanted something for my stuff. Besides, I never ride my skateboard anymore, anyway."

Lisa hung up the phone and looked over at the case again. She didn't see any real latches, just two holes on the sides of the case where the latches should be, so she figured it must be okay. She handed the case to Mike. "Yeah, well, okay then." She walked to the sink and turned. "But next time, you ask before you go trading your good stuff away. Mike took the case and nodded his head yes. The boys sat there in silence. "Well, go outside and play or something." They all got up and headed to the door. "Stay out of trouble," she added.

The boys took off out the door with the girls close behind. Joe pushed away from the table and sat in his chair. "So that's what they were up to. You can't pull anything over on you, dear."

Lisa walked up behind him and thumped him on the back of his head. "That's right, and don't you forget it."

"Ouch!" he laughed while he pulled her around the waist and sat her down onto his lap and kissed her.

CHAPTER EIGHT

THE BOYS HEADED OUT TO the backyard while they laughed and jabbered with a sigh of relief. In front of them, beyond the trees, they saw a flying saucer about ten feet off the ground. A stream of colored lights rotated around the outside of the middle of the ship. A rabbit was sitting under the saucer. The girls pointed and hollered, "Look!" The boy stopped in their tracks and stared. They all screamed and ran. The rabbit looked up and started to run off while the boys tried to catch it. Bree yelled, "Hey, what did you do that for?"

Once the rabbit was gone, the boys looked up and laughed. Rick reached up. "Chris, you left the lights on again," he scolded. He pressed a garage-door-opener button on the pole, and the stairs lowered down from the saucer to the ground. The flying saucer was the boys' clubhouse.

Mike turned and held out his hand to stop the girls. "Nuh-uh. No girls allowed."

Bree put her hands on her hips and gave a huff. "Since when?" Jenna then said, "Yeah."

Chris and Mike walked up the steps. Then Rick started up and said to the girls, "Since today, this is a Wild Boys meeting." Rick went up the steps and then the stairs started back up into the ship. Chris looked down through the doorway before it closed and yelled, "Yeah!"

The girls huffed off and went to the other side of the yard to their own playhouse. Mike watched out of the observation window of the ship until they entered their castle. Chris swiveled around in a captain's chair and turned on the stereo. Mike closed the top hatch and they went back down into the body of the ship where Rick was with the case. Chris went to a port door and opened it, then lay down on a bunk while Rick and Mike started to look the case over.

"Chris, get me the toolbox," Rick said.

Chris got up and grabbed the toolbox from the closet. He put it down next to Rick, turned on the television above the refrigerator, grabbed a soda, and lay back down on the bed. Mike asked, "I wonder what happened to the spaceship?"

Rick answered while he grabbed a screwdriver and tried to pry open the case, "I don't know."

Chris sat up. "I know, maybe the government tracked it on radar and came in last night and cleaned it up."

Rick replied, "Nah, we would've heard something, big trucks or helicopters or stuff." Rick got a skinnier screwdriver and wedged it into the seam on the front of the case. All of a sudden, the screwdriver and the case started to buzz and then, *zap, pop, zing*! Rick, Mike, and Chris jumped when the sparks flew from the screwdriver.

Chris spilled his soda. "What the heck?"

Rick looked at the screwdriver that was now burnt halfway off. "Whoa! I'm not trying that again."

Mike checked out the case. There wasn't a mark on it. "I wonder how this thing opens."

Rick thought about the case back when the alien handed it to them. "The alien put your hand on the case, Mike. So I think it's up to you."

Mike looked at the two holes in the case just big enough for his thumbs. "Maybe the latches work off of heat, or perspiration or something like that?"

Rick replied, "Be my guest, try it out." Mike was scared after seeing what it did to the screwdriver. He took a deep breath and put his thumbs into the holes of the case. The case clicked and popped open.

Chris hopped off the bed. "You got it open!"

On the top half of the case was a view screen, some buttons and lights, and a couple of switches. Off to one side were some weird writings, like instructions. On the bottom half of the case, there was a keyboard-like typewriter with different symbols on each key. To the left side of the keyboard was a plug-in connection and to the right side was a square plate like a lid.

Chris's eyes opened wide. "What is it?"

Mike replied, "It's a computer, dummy."

Rick held up the disk from around his neck. "Yeah, but what does this disk have to do with anything?"

Mike ran his fingers across the keyboard of the computer. "That disk is a program for the computer."

"I know that. I just meant, where do you put it?"

"Hmm, probably in here." He pointed to the square little patch door. Rick picked up the fried screwdriver and started to poke it into the little hatch door. Mike pushed him away. "Don't! Do you want to break it? I can get it open."

"Go ahead then, open it."

Mike looked at the switches and the buttons. He moved a few and nothing happened. Then he touched another switch and, *click*, the screen lit up. He then pushed some of the symbols on the keyboard. *Beep, beep, beep!* The symbols appeared on the screen. Then he pressed another button that was blue and the screen started to clear line by line. "Aha!"

"Aha, what?"

"Well, this seems like an alphabet keyboard just like ours, except I don't speak their language. So this is going to take me a while." He pushed on some more buttons and hit a few more switches. "A long while."

Rick got up and put his hands in the air. "Oh great! An alien crashes here, seems desperate to get rid of this stuff before he dies, then forgets to give us a translation book."

Chris started to laugh and lay back down on the bunk. Mike reached over and grabbed a pencil and paper and started to copy the symbols down off the computer. Rick went up to the observation deck to play a videogame. The rabbit came back out under the ship, while the sun traveled across the sky.

Chris and Rick were real intent on a video Ping-Pong game when the girls came running over to the spaceship. Bree threw her shoe up at the observation window and Jenna yelled, "Mom says it's time for supper if you still want to go to the movies."

Rick missed the ball because of the shoe, shut the game off, and said, "I completely forgot. Mike," he yelled, "we gotta go."

Mike closed the case and hid it under his bunk in his cubicle and then closed the compartment door. Chris lowered the steps and they ran to the house.

Lisa had a light meal of soup and sandwiches. The boys quickly washed up and changed and came back down just when Joe came into the kitchen.

Lisa was surprised. "Wow, I wish you would get ready for Sunday church that fast. Come on, sit down and eat. I don't want you filling up on junk food at the movies."

They all sat down, prayed, ate, and dropped their bowls into the kitchen sink.

Joe pecked Lisa on the cheek. "See you later, dear." He headed out the door.

The boys followed close behind, along with the girls. They all jumped into the truck. Rick asked, "We're not taking the girls, are we?"

Joe was stern. "Why not? The girls deserve a night out too, you know."

Rick frowned. "Okay, I guess so."

Joe laughed, "No, I'm just messing with you. The girls and I are going to the park and then we will probably get an ice cream at Brandies."

The girls clapped with delight. "Yay."

Joe drove into town and dropped the boys off in front of the Show Palace. Jen and Wendy were already waiting by the doors. The boys jumped out and Joe said, "Have a good time, and Rick?"

Rick turned around and walked back over to the truck. "Yeah, Dad."

Joe handed him forty dollars. "After the movie, see if the girls want to go to Brandies for an ice cream and I'll meet you there. Don't worry, we'll sit way in the back, so as not to bother you."

Rick turned a shade of red, but smiled. "Thanks, Dad." He turned to walk away.

"Wait," Joe said. He reached into the glove box and pulled out a bottle of aftershave, put it on his hands, and patted it onto Rick's face. "There, now you smell like a man. Go gettem, tiger."

Rick was really embarrassed now. "Dad!" He walked away.

Jen took Rick by the arm. "Ooh, you smell nice. Wendy and I already have our tickets."

Rick walked up to the window. "Three, please." The clerk handed him three tickets and his change. Rick passed one to Chris and one to Mike and they all went in together.

While they were waiting for the movie to start, Jen asked, "So what did you do all day?"

Rick replied, "Oh, nothing, just played video games."

Wendy asked, "Why was Police Chief Johnson out at your place this morning? I saw that he stopped you after school yesterday."

The boys didn't want to say anything about what they had seen, so Mike answered, "Yeah, that was it. We ran the stop sign."

Jen asked, "What about the plane crash?"

Chris said, "What plane crash?"

"The one you guys said you saw," she said.

Rick asked, "How did you hear about that?"

Jen laughed, "I'm a girl. I have my ways. This is a very small town, don't you know."

Rick sat up in his seat. "No, seriously, how did you find out?"

Jen laughed again. "Marie's our neighbor. She talks to my mom all the time."

Rick was relieved. "Oh yeah, that's right." Now the theater went dark and the movie started.

CHAPTER NINE

IT WAS NOW EARLY MONDAY morning at school. The paper that Mike had drawn the symbols on was on the table in the school library. Mike was sitting at the table with ten books stacked on the end and three others laid out by his paper. Mike paged through a few more books, then decided on the two that he wanted. The first bell rang. Mike checked out the two books of the thirteen that he'd gone through and headed to his locker. When he arrived, Rick was there talking to Jen. Mike hoped that Rick wouldn't slip and say anything to her about what had gone on that past weekend. He knew his brother and that he would want to make a big impression and boast.

Jen saw Mike coming down the hallway. "Hi, Mike."

Mike stepped up to open his locker. "Hi, Jen."

Jen moved over and out of his way. "Wendy has been asking about you today."

"What?"

"She was wondering if you were mad at her or something."

"When? I haven't seen her since Saturday night."

"Exactly. She told me that she said hello to you when you were walking into the library and you walked right by. It's like you didn't even notice her and that you were avoiding her."

"I wasn't avoiding her. I…I was just preoccupied, that's all."

"Well, she said if you are still interested, you could meet her after school by the flagpole bench."

All three of them started walking down the hall together. "Okay, thanks. If you see her, tell her that I will be there after school."

Rick looked at Mike. "What about our project?"

Jen looked at Rick. "What project?"

Mike answered, "Lay off. I have everything under control. I'll meet you at home when I get there."

Rick replied, "Geez," while Mike walked away to his next class.

Jen wiggled her finger into Rick's chest. "Rick, what project?"

The second bell rang. Rick opened the door for Jen and their next class. "Oh, it's just a Wild Boys thing."

It was now the end of the school day. The last bell rang and Mike ran out of the door to wait for Wendy. He thought back to the first time that he'd seen Wendy while the kids filed out from the school. It was at the school dance during the DJ playoffs. Wendy Rogers was a beautiful dark-skinned girl with brown eyes and black hair about shoulder length. She had dimples when she smiled, which she did all the time. It was so infectious, people could not help but smile at her when she came into view. There she was, across the way on the other side of the gymnasium talking to her friends. Mike danced across the room right over to her and held out his hand. "May I be enchanted by your beauty while you dance with me?" Wendy blushed and they walked to the center of the floor and the music started to play. When they started to dance, it was like they'd rehearsed it together for months. The whole school stood back to watch.

Mike noticed Wendy as soon as she came out of the door. Her long black hair floated around her soft brown shoulders while she talked to her girlfriends. Her eyes had that twinkle that made Mike swoon. Mike yelled from across the courtyard, "Wendy, over here."

Wendy walked over to Mike. "Hi, Mike, would you like to walk me home?" Mike smiled and took her backpack for her. They walked over to get his bike and started to walk out of town. "I thought you were mad at me?"

Mike shook his head and smiled. "No, never, I was just preoccupied with a Wild Boys project."

Wendy smiled and gave Mike a nudge. "Oh, you guys and your Wild Boys club. How can I compete with that?"

Mike chuckled. "You don't have to compete. You just have to push me harder to get my attention."

"You mean like this?" Wendy gave Mike a push off the sidewalk.

Mike stumbled. "No, not like that, a push with your lips."

"Oh, you bad boy, you," she laughed, to which Mike replied, "No, not a bad boy, a Wild Boy."

They continued down the road, holding hands while they talked back and forth. Mike walked Wendy up to her front door. Wendy turned and smiled and gave Mike a peck on the cheek. Mike's eyes lit up and a big smile came on his face. He handed her backpack to her and turned back to get on his bike. When Wendy opened the screen door, she turned and saw Mike pop a wheelie and wave while he rode down the road. Wendy waved to Mike with a wide smile on her pretty little face.

CHAPTER TEN

THAT NIGHT AT THE SUPPER table, Mike was daydreaming and playing with his mashed potatoes while the rest of them talked about their day. Rick said something about a paper, which reminded Chris of something that he had forgotten. "Oh, Mom, Dad, you need to sign this permission slip for me so I can go on this field trip tomorrow." He pulled out the crumpled paper from his pants pocket and handed it to his mother.

Lisa took the slip and tried to read it. "So where are you going?"

Chris sat up in his chair. "We're going to some big science exhibit in Lafayette."

Lisa read the slip. "This says you won't be back until seven o'clock and you need ten dollars."

"Yeah. The teacher said that we need to pack a lunch to take with us and the ten dollars is for McDonald's or something like that for dinner."

"Chris, why do you always wait until the last minute to give me these things?"

Joe interjected, "Maybe so you can't volunteer to go along," and chuckled.

"Oh, shut up, dear."

Mike had a thought. "Mom, as long as Chris isn't coming home until late, can I stay in town to ride home with him?"

Lisa questioned, "What are you going to do in town while you wait for your brother?"

"I need to go to the public library to find some books."

"What about supper?"

"I'll stop over at Brandies malt shop for something to eat."

"All right, but you'd both better come straight home when Chris gets in, and don't you fill up on ice cream sodas or any junk food for your dinner. Do you hear me?"

Joe laughed, "Worrywart."

Lisa turned to Joe. "Don't you start with me."

Now Rick spoke up. "Mom, can I stay too? I can help Mike at the library."

"Sure, go ahead, that will make my life easier. I'll just take the girls out after school and go shopping and grab something for us to eat. Your father can just eat his old fishing worms or something."

Joe laughed, "Ha, ha, ha, they would probably be a lot better than your leftovers. Little butter, a pinch of salt and a fry pan, yum, top it off with some ice cream, worms à la mode."

Lisa crinkled her nose at Joe and the twins shouted, "OOOH, yuck. That's gross," and they all started to laugh.

The next day, Chris was walking through the science exhibit. He and his friends were goofing around when they happened upon an exhibit that caught Chris's interest. He stopped to look. It had a bunch of different symbols and writings throughout the world and throughout time. Some of them looked similar to the ones that Chris remembered seeing on the alien computer. Chris looked at the man's name, address, and picture. He was at the university, right there in Lafayette. Chris wrote down the information in his science notebook. His friends walked back to rib him. One said, "Come on, Chris, let's go. Why are you taking notes about that crazy writing? Are you going to be a spy and write in secret code?"

He laughed at them while he was putting his pen away. "I'm coming." Chris continued on with his friends, goofing around and walking through the exhibits. "It's a secret, I'll never tell you guys about it."

One of the girls in the group said, "Oh, Chris, you're such a kidder."

Chris looked at his watch. "Hey, we need to get to the bus or it's going to leave without us if we don't hurry."

Just then an announcement came across the PA system in the exhibit hall. "All kids from Columbus

Junior High, report to the bus. All kids from Columbus Junior High, report to the bus."

"See, I told you. Come on, let's go." They all ran down the hallway to the front door.

When the bus got back into town, Chris couldn't wait to get off to tell his brothers the great news of what he had found at the exhibit. When the bus pulled into the parking lot, he saw Rick and Mike waiting for him. He stuck his head out the bus window and hollered for their attention. "Rick, Mike, I found it, I got it! It's just what we needed." With the roar of the bus engine and the brakes squealing to a stop, the two boys didn't hear a thing of what Chris had said. By the time Chris got his head back into the bus, all the kids were standing up in the aisle of the bus and pushing each other to get out the door in a hurry. Of course, Chris was in the back of the bus and was the last one to get off. When he stepped off the bottom step of the bus, Rick threw his Wild Boys jacket to him. On the bike ride home, Chris told them about his day and what he had found out at the science exhibit. He told them about the name of the man and the research of all the writings throughout history.

The next day after school, the boys came straight home to call the university to speak to the professor. Lisa was out back hanging up the laundry, so Chris watched the door while Mike dialed the phone...*dit-dit-dit-dit-*

dit-dit-dit… The phone rang and a woman answered, "Natural Science University, how may I help you?"

Mike looked at Chris to make sure that their mom was not coming back into the house. "Yes, I'm trying to reach a Professor Ungerweir."

The operator replied, "Just a moment, please." *Ring, ring* went the phone.

A man's voice came onto the phone. "Hello?"

Mike answered, "Professor Ungerweir?"

"Yes, this is he."

"My name is Mike Ramsey and I found some symbols that you might be interested in. I was wondering if my brothers and I could set up an appointment to meet with you so we could show them to you. I am really interested in what I found and would like to know what it all means."

"Well, young man, how old are you?"

"Twelve years old, almost thirteen."

"So, Mike, how do you know of me?"

"Well, my little brother Chris went to the science exhibit at the State Fair yesterday and saw your exhibit there."

"All right, now, where did you say you found these symbols and what do they look like?"

"I really can't say where, but I sure would like your input on them if you could help me. They are similar to the Bronze Age on your display at the exhibit but they're a little bit different from the Dispilio tablet, so I'm thinking that it must be older than that."

The professor was dead quiet. He was thinking about how a twelve-year-old boy was interested in the same things that he was, and when he heard him say the Dispilio tablet, he was overwhelmed with enthusiasm, because that tablet was the oldest language that modern man knew about.

"Professor, are you still there?"

"Ah, yes, yes, I'm here. All right then, how about nine o'clock on Saturday morning?"

"Sure, that will be great. My brothers and I will be there."

"Do you know how to get here, the university, that is?"

"Well, no, not really."

"Umm, do you have access to a fax machine?"

"Yeah, there's one at the Triple X Copy Store in town. We can use that one."

"All right. You go there tomorrow and I'll have the directions waiting for you there. I'll call the store for the fax number, now just give me your name and address."

"It's Mike Ramsey, 3003 Ricky Road, Columbus, Wisconsin."

"Okay, Mike Ramsey, I will see you on Saturday morning at nine o'clock."

"Thanks, Professor Ungerweir. I'll see you then, bye."

"Goodbye."

Mike hung up the phone and did a high five with Rick. "We got it, Saturday morning at nine o'clock at the university. He said he'll meet with us and look at the symbols."

Rick thought out loud, "Now all we have to do is get a ride to Lafayette."

Chris turned. "No problem, let's just go and ask Mom if she will take us there."

Rick answered, "Heck no! Mom is too nosy, let's go ask Dad."

So the boys headed out the door to find their dad. Joe was working in his shop making wooden things as usual, in his free time, which he didn't get much of these days. The boys approached their dad, all excited about going to meet with Professor Ungerweir. Rick entered first. "Hi, Dad, can we ask a favor of you for Saturday morning? It's not much."

Joe turned off his sander. "Hi, guys, what's up? What kind of favor and how much is it going to cost me?"

"It won't cost you a cent. We just want to know if you can take us to Lafayette on Saturday at nine o'clock in the morning."

"Why, what's going on in Lafayette so early in the morning? Are you going to the fair?"

That would've been a good excuse, but Rick answered, "No, we made an appointment with a professor at the university."

"What for? You guys are too young to be thinking about college."

"Well, it's a school project."

"A school project? School is out for the summer, isn't it?"

"Well, it's more like a school summer project."

Joe squinted his eyes. "Uh-huh."

"Come on, Dad, please?"

Then Mike spoke up. "Yeah, Dad, please? It's a Saturday and we will not be in your hair or in Mom's."

Joe thought about it while he looked at the boys. He was never one to deny his children an adventure or education. "All right, guys, you got a good point there. I'll take you into Lafayette to the university. But I have to check with your mother first."

The boys were all excited. "Thanks, Dad!" They headed out the door. Joe took a break and sat down with a smirk and just shook his head. The boys ran off to their spaceship to discuss what they would tell the professor.

CHAPTER ELEVEN

BY SATURDAY MORNING, MIKE HAD gone through all the books he had pulled from the library. He had about three and a half pages of notes and pictures of symbols. He was still in his room getting all the papers together and going over all his notes when he heard his dad honk the horn of the truck. Mike grabbed all the papers, stuffed them into his backpack, and ran down the stairs, slamming the bedroom door behind him. He headed out of the house at the same time that Chris and Rick arrived by the truck. The girls came out right behind him and ran to their daddy by the truck. Jenna asked, "Can we go too, please?"

Bree grabbed ahold of her daddy's leg. "Please, Daddy, please?"

Joe smiled and ran his hands down the backs of their long blonde hair. "Sure, you girls can come along. Hop in and buckle up."

At that time Lisa came out of the house and walked up to Joe. "Can I go too?" The boys looked up with a frown.

Joe gave Lisa a peck on the lips. "Sure dear, if you want to."

"I would like to, but I have to go into the shop today. I'm doing a different window display today."

"Okay, you go have your fun."

Joe and Lisa share a kiss for the road, and then Joe got into the truck and off they went, down the road to Lafayette. The boys were much relieved that their mother didn't come along with them.

When they approached the city, the girls started to gaze out the windows. They were so excited about seeing the big buildings and all the cars and the people that rushed about. They were only two when they'd left Chicago, so this was all new to them. Mike pulled out the map and the directions that he'd picked up from the copy store the day before and handed them to his dad. "Here's the directions, Dad. I thought you might need them to get us to the university." Joe glanced at it and smiled at Mike, then drove straight to the university.

He stopped the truck and the boys started to get out. "Here we are, Natural Science University, my old alma mater. Wait, what time do you boys want me to pick you up?" The boys turned and shrugged their shoulders. "Well, it is eight thirty now, and you said your appointment was at nine o'clock. What do you say the girls and I will be back here at around noon and we will all go to lunch. If you get done earlier than that, just sit on your thumbs or something. Don't go wandering off, all right?"

The boys started to walk off and waved. Rick replied, "All right, Dad, thanks. We'll be waiting." Joe revved up the truck, put it into gear, and drove away with the girls.

The three walked through the campus grounds. They saw a lot of young men and women. Some were playing games like Frisbee and catch while others were kissing and cooing under the big trees on the university lawns. Still others were studying and discussing their school projects and grades. There were some pretty girls that came walking up to the boys. When they approached, the girl on the end said, "Ooh, girls, look at the cute boys. Are you guys lost or something? Can we help you look for your class?" she giggled.

Mike spoke up, a little on the defensive. "No, we are here to see Professor Ungerweir."

The second girl bent down in front of the boys at eye level. "Oh, you mean Stinky. You go through the main entrance, turn right, and it's the first door on the left. It says Science Labs on the door. You can't miss it."

The smell of her perfume rolled around the boys and filled Rick's lungs. Rick looked at her and smiled dreamily into her eyes as she straightened up. Then he replied in a low, soothing voice, "Thank you, you were really helpful."

The girl answered, "You are quite welcome, cutie," while she caressed his chin and walked away. Rick's face turned bright red. Mike grabbed him by the arm and pulled. "Come on, Rick, let's go." Chris giggled.

They found their way to the lab and opened the door. The room smelled like bad body odor. The boys saw a man working at his desk. Chris pointed at him for his brothers. "That's him."

Mike walked forward. "Professor Ungerweir, I'm Mike."

The professor looked up from his desk and stood to greet the boys. "Yes, Mike Ramsey. How do you do?" They shook hands. "These are your brothers, I presume. Hello, boys."

Mike pulled out the paper with the keyboard symbols and explained what he had done. "This is what I am trying to figure out. Now, I got some books from the library and tried the symbol correlations, but once I thought I got one letter, the next one would be the same or a bunch of different letters in the same symbol. I just can't get a system."

The professor started to study the symbols deeply. He was really intrigued. "Where did you get this? This is fabulous." He studied some more. "May I make a copy of this? I don't believe this, this is wonderful."

Mike answered, "Sure."

The professor walked behind his desk and sat in his chair. Then he spun around and grabbed a big book from his bookcase. The boys looked at each other and sat down in the class chairs to wait. The professor started to doodle on a paper, paging through his book. He scratched his head and giggled and talked to himself. "Where did this come from?" The boys knew that he really wasn't asking them a question by the tone in his voice. "This is fantastic!" He giggled and figured some more. The boy sat patiently for about ten minutes.

Then Rick asked, "Sooo, what's up, Doc?" There was no reply. The boys looked at each other and Rick shrugged his shoulders.

Mike said, "Professor?" He waited. "Professor," he said a little louder.

The professor broke from his study. "Ah, yes, Mike."

"So can you help? Can you figure out the alphabet?" Mike walked over to the professor's desk.

The professor was all excited. "Oh no, no, no, no, I mean yes."

"What?"

"I mean no, you are wrong and yes, I can figure it out, but it's going to take some time. You see, it's not an alphabet system keyboard. It's more of a shorthand keyboard, like what a stenographer would use."

"Stenographer?"

"Yes, like what they use in the courts, stenography. You see, it is symbols for words, and different symbols together can make different words. Here, let me show you."

About two and a half hours went by while Mike and the professor worked out the symbols. Chris was bored so he fell asleep. Mike figured out one of the symbols with patience, perseverance, and the help of the professor.

Rick lifted his head up off the desk and looked at the clock. "Mike, we have to go. Dad's going be here in a little while."

Mike started to pick up his papers. "Okay, just a minute."

The professor asked, "Could you come back next week? I should have it completed by then. Let's say, Saturday morning at nine o'clock again?"

Mike answered, "Well, yeah, I guess so." The professor got up and made some more copies of all the papers that they had worked on. He handed Mike some and kept the rest for himself. Mike packed the papers away and held out his hand to the professor.

The professor shook his hand and walked the boys to the door. "Nine o'clock then, Saturday."

Mike answered, "Thanks, Professor."

The professor continued to walk with them down the hallway. "Oh, my pleasure boys. Now tell me, where did you get this from?"

Mike said, "You wouldn't believe us if we told you."

The professor answered, "Try me."

The boys looked at each other and nodded their heads as though to say, *sure, why not?* Mike looked around the campus to make sure they were alone. "From a spaceship."

The professor swirled around, holding his hands in a praying position. "I knew it! I knew it. I wasn't sure but I knew it had to be. Does anyone else know?"

Mike replied, "No, when we went back to the crash site, everything was gone." They walked through the main entrance. "Oh, there's our dad, we have to go."

Now the professor was full of questions. "No, wait!" He muddled. "Well, okay then, I'll see you next Saturday, right?"

Mike shook his hand once again. "Right." Then the boys headed to the truck. The professor went off with a skip and a twirl like a ballerina as the boys got into the truck.

Joe opened the door and watched the professor. The boys got in, and then Joe asked, "Who is that nut?"

Rick replied, "That's Professor Ungerweir."

Chris snickered, "Yeah, Stinky." The boys laughed and the girls did too.

Joe got back into the truck. "So did you find out what you wanted?"

Mike answered, "Yup."

Joe asked them where they would like to eat and the kids argued back and forth while their dad drove down the road toward the fair.

CHAPTER TWELVE

THE REST OF THE WEEK went normal. Mike was busy day and night, working on the symbols. Joe and Lisa were relaxing, sitting on the porch swing. Lisa said while looking up at the stars, "Oh, look, there's a shooting star."

Joe tilted his head. "Yup, you wouldn't see that in Chicago."

They swung for a bit and she asked, "Do you think Mike is all right?"

"Why?"

"Because school was out last Wednesday and Mike is still studying now in the summer."

"Yeah, it's what he likes to do. Don't knock it. Maybe he'll be our prodigy."

Bree and Jenna were in the living room watching TV and the phone rang. They both got up and ran for the phone. Jenna got to it first. "Hello, Ramsey residence. This is Jenna speaking."

The man on the other end answered, "Hello, Jenna, this is Professor Ungerweir. Is Mike there, please?"

"Just a minute, please," Jenna said, then yelled for her brother, "Mike, telephone." The professor had to pull the phone away from his ear when she yelled.

Joe heard her and answered from the porch, "He's in the clubhouse." Then he yelled out, "Mike, phone."

The stairway was down so Mike heard his father. "Okay, Dad." Mike came down out of the clubhouse and ran to the house. The girls were giggling and whispering back and forth to each other. Mike entered the house. "Who is it?"

Jenna handed him the phone. "It's Stinky Underwear." The girls ran off giggling and laughing.

Mike put the phone to his ear. "Hello?"

"Hello, Mike. This is Professor Ungerweir. I have done it, I think. I'm just calling to confirm for Saturday. Are you still coming?"

"Yeah, okay."

"All right, I'll be waiting, then. Just come back to the lab, I'll be there."

"Okay, bye."

"Bye-bye, see you Saturday."

Mike hung up the phone and went out to the porch to talk to his mom and dad. "Dad, can we go to the city again on Saturday?"

"I am afraid not, Mike, I have to work," Joe replied.

Mike looked at his mother. "Mom?"

"No, I have to work in the store on Saturday. Mandy's having her baby, so I'm covering her shift."

Mike didn't want to press the issue and said, "Well, no big deal." He paused, then asked, "Can we sleep in the spaceship tonight?"

Joe answered, "Yeah, sure, that's why I built it."

Mike walked away and ran upstairs. That night the boys had a meeting in their clubhouse before going to bed. Rick asked, "What's up?"

Mike answered, "Professor Ungerweir called and he said he got it completed."

Chris held up his hand for a high five. "Yay!" Not getting one, he got up and went to lie down in his bunk.

Mike continued, "The only thing is that Mom and Dad are both working on Saturday."

For a moment there was nothing but silence. Then Rick answered, "Well, no big deal. We'll just ride our bikes."

Chris sat up from his bed. "Ride! That's a long way."

Rick opened his cubicle and sat down. "It's only twenty miles or so. If we ride steady, it should only take us a couple of hours. So we'll leave at six thirty and we should have plenty of time." They all agreed and settled in for the night.

CHAPTER THIRTEEN

IT WAS SATURDAY MORNING ONCE again. The boys were up bright and early, packing a lunch and extra stuff, getting ready to leave. Joe came in, ready to go to work. "Where you boys off to?"

Chris looked at his dad. "Well, ah, we're going fishing."

Rick turned and spoke up. "Yeah, fishing."

Joe brushed his fingers through Mike's hair and messed it up as he walked out the door. "Okay, have fun."

The morning was crisp, cool, and clear. But it didn't take long for it to heat up on their long bike ride. The boys made it to the city and to the university with half an hour to spare. They rode up onto the lawn under a big tree, parked their bikes, and sat down to rest. When they got off their bikes, their legs were all wobbly. After a short time, a security guard came along to kick them off. At about that same time, the same girl that they'd met last week was walking from the other way, carrying a laundry basket.

The security guard walked up and said, "You boys can't rest here. This is university property."

Rick and the other two stood up. Rick replied, "We're not, we came here to meet with Professor Ungerweir."

Just then the girl walked up. "Yeah, Starchy, leave them alone. They came to see Stinky." The security guard walked away, shaking his head and mumbling to himself.

Rick turned to the girl with a smile. "Thank you."

The girl sweetly smiled back. "Anytime, cutie, any time." She walked away while the boys admired the wiggle in her walk. They took a deep breath and started off to the lab to see the professor. When they opened the door, they saw a very tall man with long arms standing by the window, looking out. He had on a white lab coat with his back turned to the boys. The boys started to feel a little puzzled.

Mike stepped forward. "Hello, is the professor here?"

The tall man answered in a monotone, "The professor is not here. May I help you?"

The boys walked in a little closer. Mike said, "Well, he was working on a project for us and he was supposed to be here."

"Yes, what project?" the tall man asked, still facing the window.

As they walked closer, he pulled his hands out of the lab-coat pockets. Rick noticed his hands, and the color of his skin was blue. Mike started to say, "Well, it was…"

Rick grabbed Mike back and whispered, "Mike, it's an alien."

Before he could say anything more, the alien turned around and looked at them with his big eyes that had no visible white in them. "Where is the case?"

The boys scattered and fanned out between and behind the tables in the room. Mike yelled back, "Where is the professor?"

The alien put his hands on the table and leaned forward. "You will come with me."

Chris answered, "No way, man."

Rick said, "Let's get out of here."

The alien tried to grab them as they all ran out the door together and down the hallway. The alien was closing in from behind them. When they got to the end of the hallway, Rick saw the alien closing in, and yelled, "Break!" All three boys split off into different directions. The alien stopped and stood there for a few seconds, not knowing which one to follow. Then he turned around and went the other way.

All three boys made it back to their bikes and started pedaling down the street. Mike asked, "Where did he go?"

Rick answered, "Who cares, let's just get out of here." Right at that time, a red spaceship like car cut broadside in front of them. They slammed on their brakes to stop. They saw the alien glaring at them. Rick pointed. "Come on, this way."

The boys took off across the campus lawn and under the trees. They pulled back onto the street on the other side of the campus with the alien coming in close behind. They made a bunch of different turns and maneuvers with the alien either cutting them off or being right behind them. The boys headed down a back-alley walkway and turned down the street with the alien right behind. In front of them, the street was blocked by a moving van with a car parked in front of it. There was only three feet of space in the street to get through. The boys thought they had it made. Rick yelled, "All right, break." Rick split off to the left, cutting across the lawn under the low trees. Mike swung over and squeezed through the three-foot space in the road. Chris split to the right, across the other side of the moving van. At that time, the movers were walking out of the truck carrying a table.

Chris shouted, "Look out!" He ducked his head and continued to ride toward the movers. The movers saw him coming and instinctively raised the table up into the air. Chris rode under the table while one of the movers started to yell, "Hey, watch it." Then he saw the red car driving straight for the center of the van. The car flew up and over the top of the van and the mover dropped the table and pointed. "Wow, did you see that? John, did you see that?"

John yelled, "Hey!"

The mover replied, "That car just flew over the top of the van."

John replied, "Yeah right, you're lucky you didn't break this table. Now pick it up and be careful."

The boys came back together and Mike started to have trouble with his bike chain again. Rick and Chris didn't notice that Mike was falling behind when they turned the corner and headed down the hill. The spaceship flew over Mike and followed the other two. Rick and Chris went through an intersection, not noticing the dead-end sign. When the road turned they slammed on their brakes before running into a three-foot stone wall with a chain-link fence on top of it. The alien stopped right behind them. They were out of breath and couldn't think of running at that moment. The spaceship hovered one foot off the ground while the hatch opened. The top half of the ship lifted up and slid down the back of the ship to the ground. The tall alien got out and walked over to the two boys.

He saw the disk around Rick's neck. "Give me the disk." Rick was worn out, scared, and out of ideas. He handed the disk over to the alien. The alien looked at it and put it into his lab-coat pocket. "Now, where is the case?" The boys didn't reply. The alien pulled a small rope out of his pocket.

At that same time, Mike came down the sloping road and around the curve. He was still having trouble with his bike. His chain jumped off, leaving him without any brakes. Mike hit the back of the spaceship, which acted like a ramp and propelled him into the air. He yelled to his brothers, "Look out!" The boys saw him coming in and ran for cover. The alien only had enough time to turn around and put his arms up before Mike came crashing down on top of him. The alien crashed to the ground while Mike jumped and rolled to safety across the grass.

Chris looked over with amazement. "Whoa, that was radical, Mike."

Mike stood up, looked, and walked back over. "I was going to sneak up behind him but I couldn't stop. Is he dead?"

Rick went over and felt the alien's big vein on his collar bone. "I don't think so, he's just out cold." Rick reached into the lab-coat pocket and pulled the disk back out and put it back around his neck.

Mike picked up his bike and replaced the chain back onto the sprocket. "Well, let's go." He started to roll his bike away.

Rick quickly said, "No, wait a minute. Chris, hand me that rope." Chris picked up the alien's rope and handed it to him. Rick started to tie the alien up with his own rope.

Mike looked a little confused. "What are you doing, let's go."

Rick grabbed Mike by the arm with an angry look. "If we go and let him get away, we have no proof. Besides, when he wakes up, he's going to be pretty angry, radio his friends, and then we'll really have fun. Now help me tie him up and put him into his ship."

Now that they had him tied up, they rolled him into the spaceship. Even though it was hovering one foot off the ground, it didn't move. They tried to close the lid but it wouldn't budge. It seemed like it was being held in place by something but nothing was there that they could see.

Chris scratched his head. "Now what?"

Mike looked at the cover of the hatch and noticed that there was an opening that looked like the holes on the side of the case. "Try that." Rick put his fingers into the hole and, *buzz*, the lid started to close.

Mike went back to get his bike. "I wish the professor was here."

Rick picked up his bike. "Well, let's go get the police."

While the other two went for their bikes, Chris put his hand on the spaceship to fix his shoelace. The ship moved over and Chris fell onto the ground. "Hey, what the?" Chris got back up. "Guys, look at this." The two turned around and saw Chris pushing the hovercraft around in a big circle with only two fingers.

Rick dropped his bike. "That gives me an idea." He started to take off his shoelaces. "Mike, open the hatch." He tied his laces together and took off his belt. "Give me your belts and shoelaces. We're taking this baby home." They tied all the strings together and closed them up into the hatch.

CHAPTER FOURTEEN

DOWN THE BACK ROADS AND out of the city, the boys were pulling the spaceship behind their bikes toward home. It was a long morning but the house was soon in sight. The boys smiled at the sight of their house. Rick said, "Too bad we couldn't have flown it home."

Mike asked, "I thought we were going to call the cops?"

"You want to find out about the professor, don't you?"

"Well, yeah."

"Well then, we'll find out, then we can call Jack. Chris, go open the garage door and move the Ping-Pong table." Chris handed his shoestring rope to Rick and zoomed off ahead. When they pedaled into the driveway, Chris opened the garage door. Mike and Rick stopped and turned the ship around and backed it into the garage. Rick put his finger into the keyhole and opened the hatch while Mike closed the garage door. The alien was still stunned but was starting to come to.

Chris asked, "What do we do with him?"

Rick looked around the garage. "Let's tie him up over there in that corner to the chair." While they were tying him up, they heard their mother's minivan drive up. "It's Mom, home for lunch." Rick started to leave for the house. Chris grabbed a blanket and threw it over the alien's head.

Mike stood by the door. "I'll see you guys later. I'm going to stay here for a while to keep an eye on this guy. Make sure Mom doesn't come out here."

Both of the boys said at the same time, "Uh, duh," and left the garage.

When they entered the house, Chris waved. "Hi, Mom, home for lunch?"

Lisa pulled her head out of the fridge. "Hi, guys, have you had lunch yet? I had to come home for some supplies for my next window display. So where's Mike?"

Rick stated, "I think he went over to Mr. Rogers' to see when he needs us to bale."

"Well, he could have called him," she said. The boys shrugged their shoulders.

Rick answered, "Then he wouldn't be able to see Wendy."

"Oh yes, that's right, how silly of me. All right, wash up and I'll make you some sandwiches before I go." The boys went to wash while their mother made some sandwiches.

When they came back down, Rick asked, "Where are the girls?"

Lisa put the sandwiches on the table. "Oh, they are over at Bonnie's." Then she went over to her purse and pulled out a bunch of papers and handed them to Rick. "Here, give these papers to Mike. They came in yesterday morning at the copy store. Andy was nice enough to bring them over to the shop." Rick looked over the papers and his eyes got really big. Lisa was curious about the papers and now, with the look on Rick's face, she wondered what they were all about. "So what are those papers all about?"

Rick replied, "Oh nothing, it's just papers for his summer-school project." Rick quickly ate a sandwich and gulped down his milk. He got up from the table and headed for the door. "Thanks, Mom. Come on, Chris, let's go." Chris drank his milk and grabbed a couple of sandwiches and they headed out the door. Lisa sat back and pondered, and then she smiled to herself and said out loud while shaking her head, "Boys."

The two went back to the garage and opened the side door. When they arrived, they didn't see Mike anywhere and they got this eerie feeling. Just then a big gust of wind blew through the garage door as a cloud shadowed the sun. Mike walked up behind them and put his hand on Rick's shoulder. "Boo." Both of the boys almost jumped out of their skin.

Rick turned with a fright. "Ah, where were you?"

Mike held up the metallic case and laughed, "Gotcha, I went to the clubhouse for this." They walked in and Mike set the case down onto the workbench. He popped the case open and grabbed his papers. They heard their mom start up the minivan and drive away.

Rick handed Chris the papers from the copy store. "Here, check these out. Andy gave them to Mom for you.

"Oh cool, the professor faxed these over." Mike sat down with the papers to look them over. Chris went over to check on the alien. He was still under the sheet. Then he went to the spaceship and climbed into the seat to look it over. While Rick was helping Mike, Chris put his finger on a light in the spaceship, then on a switch. Mike glanced over at the spaceship. "I wouldn't touch that, Chris. The ship might take off."

Chris scoffed, "Don't worry, I won't." Chris put his finger over another light. The ship started to hum and the metal tools started to shake off the walls of the garage.

Mike yelled, "Chris!"

Chris quickly pulled his finger away from the light. "Okay!" He was scared now to touch anything. "I'm sorry." His hands were shaking but he didn't want his brothers to see, so he put his hands under his butt and sat on them.

A few minutes went by and Mike got up and went over to the ship. He looked at his papers, then at the panel of the ship. Chris climbed out and Mike reached over and put his finger on a button. He closed his eyes and pushed the button. The other two backed away. The ship started to hum really loudly, as if it was winding down, and then it lowered to the ground. Mike opened his eyes and smiled. "There."

Chris bent down and tilted his head and looked at the ship. "What did you do now? You broke it."

Mike then climbed into the cockpit. "No I didn't, I shut it off. Get me some tape and a Magic Marker." Rick went to the cabinet, pulled open the drawer, and got out some tape and a Magic Marker. He handed them to Mike, then climbed into the other side of the ship. Mike started to label all the symbols above each switch and light. On/Off/Hatch lock/Booster thrust/Laser/Auto computer/Sub hatch/Shield.

Rick sat back in the seat and looked over at Mike. "Well now, Captain, how does all this work?"

Mike pointed out all the controls. "Once it's turned on, everything works off the joystick and the speed control is over here. These buttons are for all the basics. The speed override is the pedal on the floor."

Chris laughed, "Oh, I get it, air brakes."

Rick commented, "Yeah, it's kind of like putting the Nintendo with Dad's truck."

Mike got out of the ship and went back to work on the computer keyboard in the case sitting on the workbench. "Right." He pushed a few more buttons and the little square door of the case opened up. "Rick, hand me that disk." Rick took the disk off from around his neck and handed it to him. Mike put it into the computer and closed the disk door. The screen lit up with a simple display. Mike pushed a few keystrokes and the screen went wild. Mike got all excited and started to jump up and down and turn in circles. "I got it! I got it." He typed in a couple more commands and a video popped on. "Whoa, oh wow, this is great, I can't believe it."

Rick was studying the inside of the spaceship while Chris was watching the alien. Chris sat on a swivel chair and was spinning around while twirling a tennis racket in his hands. "Wow what, what can't you believe?"

Mike was all excited. "Come look at this, you won't believe it either."

Rick got out of the spaceship and went over to see what Mike was ranting about. "What, so you're playing with the computer, big deal."

Rick walked over and Mike pressed a couple keys for the video to replay so the other two could watch. "Here, watch this." The three of them watched while Mike explained, "It has something to do with Earth and some other planets around here. See, there's our alien friend, the dead one. That looks like a major war on his planet." Mike pointed at the screen. "Now watch, see that? That's our solar system and that one flashing is Earth."

Chris said, "How do you know?"

Mike continued, "Because we just got done studying that in school, so we could look at the stars all summer. I do remember some things, you know."

Rick looked at Mike. "So what's it all about?"

Mike typed a little more. "Here it comes." A bunch of stuff started to print out onto the screen in English.

Chris looked. "What the heck?"

Rick started to read the printout, mumbling to himself out loud throughout the reading. "Blah, blah, blah, Earth/hydrogen/oxygen/vegetation/population/class G development/suitable for colonization. Mineral, blah, blah. Defense, nuclear only. So what does this all mean? It doesn't make any sense to me."

Mike said, "I don't know either, but it said suitable for colonization."

Chris added, "Maybe they're telling us that they want to be our neighbors?"

Rick replied, "I don't think they want to be our neighbors. According to that first part of the video, the war part, I think it looks like they want to take over and that's why our dead alien friend is dead. He was probably taking this case to his people, to show them what they were doing."

Chris asked, "What would you do if they came here?"

Rick replied, "I know what I would do. I would get Dad's shotgun and..." He turned. "As a matter of fact, we can find out what it means right now."

Chris asked, "How?"

Rick walked over to the gun case in the garage. He got the keys off the top of the case and unlocked the door. "Chris, take the sheet off the alien's head." Chris went over and took the sheet off of the alien, while Rick pulled the shotgun from out of the cabinet.

Mike turned around. "What are you going to do?"

Rick walked over by the alien and loaded the shotgun in front of him. The alien's eyes looked up with fear back at Rick. Rick put another shell in the gun. "We'll make him talk."

Chris scoffed, "He doesn't know what that is, remember, he's not from around here."

Rick put the last shell into the magazine. "Oh, he knows, it's not as nice as a laser blaster or a ray gun, but he gets the point. Yeah, it's a little old-fashioned but effective." Rick pumped the shell into the chamber and the alien cringed and started to sweat. Rick stood in front of the alien like a soldier, with the gun at left arm position. "Now tell us what we want to know."

The alien looked into Rick's eyes, then at the gun, and back again at Rick. His face then change from a scared look to a grin and his eyes looked up at the ceiling. All of a sudden, they heard a scream of a noise and a big gust of wind rolled under the garage door. The boys spun around and looked out the window. There in front of the garage door was a white spaceship hovering two feet away from the garage. Their hearts jumped and started to pound like they were going to come out of their chests. Chris's voice quivered as he asked, "What do we do now?" He looked very scared. His face was white as a ghost. Mike closed the case and put it down behind the bench, out of sight.

CHAPTER FIFTEEN

RICK WENT TO THE MIDDLE of the garage door and pushed the gun into the cross-iron of the door to open it up. "Hide! Mike, Chris, hide somewhere so they can't see you." Chris grabbed a roll of duct tape and put a strip across the alien's mouth. Then he ducked down behind the back of the Ping-Pong table in the garage. Mike left out the side door of the garage. Rick slowly opened the door as high as he could reach while still holding the shotgun in the doorframe. The spaceship opened and two aliens got out. They had the same color of skin as the one that they had captured from the other ship. The aliens started to talk to each other in their own language.

Alien One said, "The signal came from here, so he must have it."

Alien Two, "Look, it's only a kid."

"Hey, let's have some fun with this kid. Let's scare the pants off of him, we don't get to do this very often."

"What? Oh, I get it, yeah, it's been ages since we had that kind of fun."

"I mean, look at him, he's already scared. We'll pull out our lasers, yell and scream a lot, and watch him run. He's only a kid, what can he do?"

Alien Two grinned. "Yeah, this should be a kick." Alien Two reached in and pushed a button, and then both of them reached in and pulled out laser guns. They held them up and pointed them to the sky. Then a very strange look came over their faces. They squinted their big oblong eyes and scowled their lips. Rick's eyes got really big. Alien Two dropped his laser from the skyward position and pointed it at the garage. Then he said in English, "Okay, kid, we know you have the case..."

Before the alien could say another word, Rick dropped the shotgun down from the garage door and took aim and said to the alien, "Say your prayers, blue brains." Rick pulled the trigger on the gun and, *BANG*, shot the laser out of his hand and peppered his arm with buckshot. The laser went flying back into the yard as Rick pumped another shell into the chamber of his gun and aimed at the other alien. His brothers' mouths dropped open and they were dumbfounded, not knowing what to do. Mike ran out from the side of the garage with a garden hose and Chris opened the other garage door and ran out with his tennis racket.

Alien One raised his hands and quickly threw his laser into his buggy while the other alien climbed into his seat in extreme pain. Alien Two shouted to his partner in their alien language, "Let's get out of here!" Alien One took a look back at the boys and jumped into the spaceship and quickly closed the hull. Rick fired a second round into the windshield of the spacecraft but it was too late. The shot ricocheted up into the air. The ship turned a hundred and eighty degrees and, *woosh*, up it went. It was out of eyesight in a matter of seconds. When the ship got into outer space, Alien Two was smacking Alien One in the head with his good arm. "He's only a kid, what can he do, oh, ouch." The alien was in great pain and grabbed his arm, or what was left of it.

Back on the ground, Mike and Chris yelled, "Hurray," while Rick went back into the garage, put the shotgun away, and got into the spaceship that they'd saved from the aliens.

Mike dropped the garden hose and walked over to the ship. "What are you doing, Rick? I hope you're not going to do what I think you're going to do?"

Rick started up the ship and it rose up off the garage floor and hovered. "We are going after them. Now both of you get in. We don't have time to stay here and talk about it. We have to go now before it's too late and they get away."

Mike said, "What, are you crazy? We can't go after them."

Rick looked Mike square in the eyes. "If we don't go after them, they might come back down here with more of them and destroy everything, us, Mom, Dad, the whole town, maybe even the earth. Do you want to just sit here and wait to see if they will come back? Then by that time it'll be too late. No one we tell will believe us, so we have to do something about it, just the three of us. Are you both with me or do I have to do this myself? I'm going to do it and I mean now, right now."

Mike responded in a concerned voice, "But you don't know how to fly this thing."

"I think I can do it. You marked all the controls and the buttons and everything, right?"

"Yeah, but I don't know if I marked them correctly. What if I didn't? What if it's all wrong?"

"Well, we have to try some time and now is as good a time as any. It is a chance we will have to take and now is the time to take it, you with me? 'Cause I'm going."

"Okay, okay, wait a minute." Mike grabbed the computer from behind the workbench and jumped into the back. Chris was looking at the alien's laser lying on the ground. "Come on, Chris, let's go."

Chris dropped the laser and wiped the blue blood off of his fingers onto his pants. "Yuck!" He ran over to the ship and jumped into the seat next to Rick. Rick closed the lid and turned on the shields. Chris put his hand by the light like he had before and asked, "Now?"

Rick replied, "Now!" Chris covered the sensor with his finger and the ship started to hum louder and higher, real fast. Then the ship topped out and was quiet. Rick gave a thumbs-up sign while Chris and Mike gave thumbs up right back. Rick clicked the switch for pilot central control so he could drive. He put his hands on the stick. As soon as he grabbed the stick, the ship zoomed almost straight up through the roof of the garage. The garage exploded as they zoomed up and away. In a matter of seconds, they were in outer space. Mike saw an outlet between the middle of the two seats that looked like the same receptacle as the computer. He pulled the receptacle cord up and noticed the symbol, which matched the one on the computer. He opened the case and plugged it into the computer of the ship.

Chris looked down at the view of Earth getting smaller and then looked at Rick. "Wow, now what?"

Rick replied, "What do you think we're going to do up here in outer space? We are going to find those guys."

"How?"

Mike pushed a few keyboard buttons on the computer. "Turn fifteen degrees, that way." He pointed into the dark sky speckled with stars. "Just be careful, really careful."

Rick turned the ship and took off. "I will, I will, I got the hang of it now."

Chris said, "Yeah, there's no garages up here. We're only going 90,000 miles an hour, punch it, are we even moving?" Rick bumped up the speed.

Mike watched the computer, then yelled, "Brake!" Rick hit the brakes and stopped within yards of the little white ship. The boys could see that Alien One was patching up the other alien's arm with bandages. Alien Two looked out the window and Chris smiled and waved at him.

Alien Two turned to the other. "Look."

Alien One continued to wrap the bandage around his arm. "Look at what?"

Alien Two started to smack him with his good arm and then pointed. "Look, you dummy, look." Alien One turned and saw the boys in the red spaceship, almost nose to nose. "Shoot them."

Alien One pushed the button for the lasers and a light came on. "Uh, I can't."

"Why not?"

"I forgot to recharge the laser rods."

Alien Two started to hit him again. "You dummy. You know you are supposed to recharge before every mission. That's your job. You always forget, every time."

Alien One was trying to stop the other alien from hitting him. "Okay, okay, I forgot. What do we do now?"

Chris pressed the button marked laser and a button came up from under Rick's thumb and Chris's thumb, too. A handle popped out of the back wall by Mike and three guns came out of the hull of the ship, two in the front and one in the back. A crosshair sight lit up on the window of the craft. The aliens' eyes got very large and fearful as they floated nose to nose with the red ship.

"Let's get out of here," the alien said while he grabbed the stick, and, *zoom*, they took off over the top of the boys' ship.

Chris said, "Go get them, Rick. We mean business now."

Rick pulled on the stick. "All right, hold on, guys, we're in for the ride of our lives. Those creatures don't know who they're messing with. We're the Wild Boys." Rick banked the ship almost upside down and backward on its side and zoomed after them. Mike kept his eye on the computer radar screen.

He saw three other blips come onto the screen, coming toward them. "We got company, guys. Put the coffee pot on, this is going to be a long visit." As soon as he said that, *zoom*, the three ships whizzed past their ship, looking like streaks of light.

Rick asked, "What the heck was that?"

Mike grabbed the laser handle and took aim in the direction of all three of the ships. The three ships turned around and came up behind them. They started to close in on them. Mike fired and grazed one of the ships as they passed them by like they were standing still. Chris fired at one and hit the ship's back end. The ship veered off to the right and a white light, out of nowhere, like lightning, hit the alien ship and blew it apart into a million pieces.

Mike said, "Good shot, Chris."

Chris turned around. "I didn't do that."

Rick closed in on the runaway ship that they were chasing and took aim. The ship dropped down and another lightning flash came from out of nowhere, blowing that ship apart. The two remaining ships closed in, head on. Rick and Chris fired as they flew by. Mike fired and missed. He saw them start to turn around. Another lightning flash flew over the boys' ship and another ship was destroyed. The last remaining ship came up on their rear. Mike took aim and pulled the trigger. Nothing happened; the laser light came on. "I'm out, Rick, do something. I don't have any more ammo or whatever this stuff is called."

Rick shouted, "Hang on!" He slammed on the brakes and pulled up like in the movie *Top Gun*. The last ship went whizzing by. Rick pulled the ship back down and zoomed in on the other ship. Chris fired and missed while the ship veered off to the left. Then his laser light came on after he fired. Rick fired and missed when the ship veered to the right and swung around to get behind the boys once again. Rick swerved the ship and rolled around, trying to lose the last ship, but the spaceship with the alien stayed right behind them and closed in on the boys' ship.

Mike watched. "Rick, he's getting closer, do something, now!"

"I know, I'm trying but I can't shake him." Rick quickly dropped the ship downward. The alien sighted up the little red ship and put his finger on the trigger. In a split second before he pushed the trigger, a beam of light shot over the top of the boys' ship. They instinctively ducked and looked behind them to see the last ship explode into a fiery light show of big sparks and a million pieces.

Chris asked, "What the heck was that?"

Mike looked on the computer screen. The radar showed a large blob on the screen. "Rick, look out!"

Rick looked out ahead of him in the window and slammed on the brakes. In front of their little red ship was a mothership. It was as big as a large metropolis city, coming up fast. The ship came closer while Rick spun the little ship around. Mike said, "Let's get out of here. Hurry, Rick, move it!"

CHAPTER SIXTEEN

RICK TRIED TO ENGAGE THE controls to speed away. The lights flickered and went out and the stick had no control. Rick said, "I can't, I don't have any control of the ship. All the buttons are jammed, they don't work. It's like the ship is in total lockdown."

Chris turned around and looked out the window. "We're being pulled into the mothership."

Mike turned to look. "I guess this is it. Mom's sure going to be mad at us now."

The huge ship opened a big door and the little red ship was swallowed up. Once inside, the boys looked at the landing pads. The lights inside the bay were all out except for the one pad that they were drawn to. They looked up at the bay windows, outside of the bay area. There were dozens of aliens up in the control windows looking down at them or going about their business. There were other spaceships inside the mothership, all sitting on their pads. The big bay door closed while their ship was placed down onto a pad and rotated. White gases and lights started to surround the ship. The gas encircled the ship while little lightning sparks scattered and danced on the ship. The ship's hull cracked open all by itself and the gases filled the ship. The boys started to feel tingly all over as their hair stood out on their heads. Chris looked at the other two and pointed and started to laugh. "You two look funny," he said in a high and squeaky voice.

Mike looked at Chris. "So do you, Chris. I wouldn't be laughing." The lights and gases went down and the boys sat, waiting for what would happen to them next. While they looked around, Mike saw a symbol on the bay door. "Look, I've seen that symbol before. He closed the case and on the top of it was that same symbol. Mike turned to Rick. "Rick, open the hatch, these are the good guys." Rick opened the hatch and they stepped out of the ship. When they did, the bay door opened and fifteen armed guards walked out. They lined up on both sides of the door. Then three very well-dressed aliens in silver robes walked in.

The aliens bowed to the boys and the boys bowed back. Then the tallest one said, "Welcome, we are so sorry that our colleague had involved you three in our endeavor of peace."

Rick waved his hand. "Hey, no problem."

"Do you have the case with you and the disk?" the alien asked.

Mike turned around and unplugged the case and pulled it out of the ship. "Yeah, we have it. It's right here," he said and handed it to the alien. "Here you go, sir." The alien took the case and handed it to another. The other alien, who was an aide, walked off with it very quickly. Then the robed one turned back to the boys. "Thank you. We are very grateful for your insight and for your trust. Come with me, we will talk." The aliens turned and walked to the door. The boys just stood there, taking in all of what had just happened to them. The aliens turned around when they approached the door and waited for the boys to walk with them. Mike nudged his brothers. "Where else do we have to be?" They started to walk slowly toward the door. Once through the door, the aliens paired up with the boys. The boys were looking around at all the other aliens working in the enormous complexity of the ship. The second and third alien proceeded to take Rick and Chris on a tour of the ship. Alien One walked with Mike and explained about the case. "I know you have been wondering what is so important about that case."

Mike answered, "It's about interplanetary war, isn't it?"

"No, not exactly. It's about interplanetary peace. You see, our man was a diplomat observer on Dayson One. It was a newly colonized planet for our society. Once the Daysons learned our technology, they were power-hungry and planned to conquer and put a few planets into slavery for their own greed. Our man had all the information in that computer and that disk. He was trying to escape but was found out."

Mike asked, "So what will you do now that you have it? The information, I mean."

The alien and Mike walked over to the window of the bay. Mike saw about twenty-five fighter ships leaving the mothership. "You see, we are already on the way to stop them. Now we know where and whom they will attack, so we can control and seize them before they move any further. We will round up the Daysons and put them back on their own planet with no outside interference. We will also take away all our technology and their means of space travel. This will give them centuries upon centuries to think about their actions." While they walked, they talked and ended up looking out a window at all the stars.

The second and third alien entered the room with Rick and Chris. The boys came running up to Mike, all excited, and rambled. Chris showed Mike. "Mike, look what we got. They are so cool. I like it here. My friends can't get anything like this stuff on Earth." Chris showed him a flashlight that was very bright but didn't have a lightbulb or batteries to operate it. "Isn't this cool? It also has a lifetime warranty." Then he showed him a musical instrument that played tones with a touch of a finger. "It's also a language translator and a recorder." The third alien handed the same items to Mike. "Aren't these neat? No one else on Earth will have these, just us," Chris added.

Mike looked at the items. "Yeah, real neat." Then he turned to the alien. "Can we keep them?"

The second alien said, "Yes, of course you boys may have them. We trust you will keep them in good faith. It is also the least that we can do for you, having involved you with our troubles."

Mike nodded his head. "Thank you, very much. We will keep them with pride."

The three aliens told them to wait there while they left the room. Rick and Chris started to tell Mike all about the ship. "Do you know that there are over 190,000,000 people on board this ship?"

Mike said, "You mean like us, from Earth?"

"No. I mean aliens. Aliens of all different races, different planets. They have schools and hospitals, shuttles and planetariums too. This place is like forty times the size of Texas," Rick replied. He continued to talk for a little while longer, not noticing the little blue marble coming into view of the window. Then the aliens returned to the room.

The alien that accompanied Mike walked over. "It's time for you to return to your world. Our shuttle officer will take you back to Earth and you will no longer be involved in our problems. We enjoyed your visit with us and appreciate all that you did for our people."

Mike had to ask. "Wait, what about Earth? What about our planet? Can't you help our planet, our world in its peace and stuff?"

The alien reached into his robe and pulled out a small book. "Here is a book of our bylaws for our society. This will help you to understand why."

Chris interjected, "What about our garage? Our dad is going to kill us when he sees what happened to the garage. What are we going to tell him? They won't believe us when we tell them about all this stuff. I bet we'll be grounded all summer."

The alien put his arm around Mike and started to walk the boys out. "You see, your world is not yet ready for submission into our advanced society. Once encountered, they would want to be just like the Daysons. Your planet would want to rule and conquer and destroy, just as they did in their past. You are at war right now and have problems and troubles with your own world neighbors. Yes, it will take many more years before your planet is ready. We will meet again, Mike, but it will take your world five hundred years before they will come to a peaceful understanding. If they do not, your world will fall into its own self-destruction. We will be watching and waiting for when your world is ready."

Mike smiled. "I guess you are right. We are new to this stuff, so I guess you know what you're talking about."

The boys shook hands with the aliens. They walked back to the ship's hangar where a shuttle was warming up. When they arrived, the boys saw the bay was full of aliens of all different races. Before they got on board, an aide brought in some boxes and handed them to the three aliens. The three aliens stood in front of the three boys and opened the little boxes. Inside each was a little silver case. They opened them up and pulled out a medal from each case. The medals were little silver disks on a glass-like chain. They put the medals on the boys and shook their hands again. All the aliens clapped and cheered. The boys climbed aboard the shuttle ship and waved goodbye. The shuttle closed its door and pulled off the platform, while all the aliens filed out of the bay. The lights started to flash, the bay was cleared, and the big bay door started to open. Once the door was open, the shuttle went out into space.

CHAPTER SEVENTEEN

THE BOYS LOOKED OUT THE window and watched the big ship disappear into the darkness. Moments later, they turned to watch while the moon went whizzing by and Earth started to grow bigger and larger as they approached. The shuttle slowed down when it hit the atmosphere. The outside of the ship hazed up with a brilliant glow. It zoomed in, stopped, and hovered over their house for a bit to cool down.

Lisa heard the noise that the shuttle made. She saw it fly over the house and thought at first that she was just having a long day. Meanwhile, Joe was looking at the damage done to the garage door and roof with Jack and the professor. Lisa hollered, "Joe, Jack! It's a spaceship! Come quick. It's over the back of the house." The house vibrated when the shuttle started to move and the twins came running down the stairs, all a-fright. By the time that Jack and Joe turned around, the ship moved toward open ground and landed in the field behind the house. Jack, Lisa, and Joe went running out back behind the house to take a look.

The door of the shuttle slowly opened just as they all came around the corner of the house. The boys were waving and saying goodbye to the shuttle driver. Jack pulled out his gun and Joe pushed his arm down and pointed. "Look, it's the boys." Jack tipped his hat back and scratched his head. The professor went running out into the field.

Lisa said, "Well, I'll be." She started to run out to the boys as the shuttle lifted up, hovered, turned, and took off. Joe and Jack went running out too. The boys waved and ran toward them.

The professor went running past the boys, waving and jumping at the shuttle. "Wait! Take me, take me," he yelled.

They all hugged each other while their parents murmured, "Where were you? Are you all right? What happened? What did they do to you? How, why, who are they?" On and on they went, with so many questions and concerns.

Professor Ungerweir came back to the group and Mike gave him a big hug. "I'm so glad that you are all right."

The professor smiled. "Yes, it was just a little bump on the head."

Rick answered their concerns as they started to walk. "Well, you probably won't believe us when we tell you."

Mike interjected, "Yeah, it's a long story."

Chris turned to his mother. "We're fine, Mom, what's for supper? I'm starved."

"You mean to tell me they didn't even feed you? Well, I never."

The girls arrived to the gathering just as a silence filled the air. Joe said with awe, "Starved? Well, Lis, let's get these space adventurers something to eat." They all started to walk toward the house. "So what do you young adventurers want to eat?"

The boys looked at each other and all replied at the same time, "Galactic pizza."

Chris added, "Yeah, that sounds good."

Everyone laughed while they walked and chatted through the field. The boys were all talking at the same time, telling of their adventure, each in their own words. Mike was walking with the professor. "Oh, Professor, I got something for you." He pulled out the book from his pocket and handed it to the professor. "It's like their Bible. I want you to have it." The professor started to cry with joy.

Rick looked at his dad and pulled his arm before going into the house. He waited until everyone else was inside. "Dad?" he said with a concerned look.

Joe sat down on the steps of the house and looked at Rick, putting his hand on his shoulder. "What is it, Rick, what's the matter?"

Rick looked down at the ground. "Sorry about the garage."

Joe just grinned a big grin and put his arm around Rick's neck and pulled him in for a hug. "That's okay, Rick. You guys had us worried. As long as you boys are safe, that's what matters. We can always build a new garage, but we can never make another you."

Chris stepped in the kitchen doorway and held up a pizza box and yelled, "Rick, pizza."

Joe messed up Rick's hair, stood up, and they walked up the steps to go into the house.

www.ingramcontent.com/pod-product-compliance
Lightning Source LLC
Chambersburg PA
CBHW020529120726
47904CB00003B/1012